The Astral Plane

Stories of Cuba, the Southwest and Beyond

Teresa Dovalpage

Printed in the United States of America

Teresa Dovalpage

The Astral Plane: Stories of Cuba, the Southwest and Beyond

print ISBN: 978-1-60801-076-9

e-book ISBN: 978-1-60801-078-3

Library of Congress Control Number: 2011940455

cover art by Carlos Daniel J. Vázquez

University of New Orleans Press

unopress.org

Acknowledgments

I want to express my deepest gratitude to Lorraine Lopez and Ileana Pelaez for agreeing to read this book before publication and for helping me immensely with their suggestions and support. ¡Gracias!

Earlier versions of some stories were published in *Rosebud* ("Seven Pennies for Yemayá"), *Mija Magazine* ("A Virgin for Cachita") and *Label me Latin@* ("Goodbye, Santero"). The first part of the novella "Menina and the *Chupacabras*" was published as "Dos Gardenias" in *Afro Hispanic Review*.

To my friend and Maestra
Lorraine Lopez, with cariño
and great admiration.

Contents

THE ASTRAL PLANE

STORIES OF CUBA, THE SOUTHWEST AND BEYOND

The Astral Plane

I: If anything were to happen

Silence fell over the Cosmic Brotherhood members like a heavy fleece blanket. All eyes were closed, all necks tensed, all breaths on hold. The moment of a manifestation had come. Maestro exhaled loudly, opened his thin, sinewy arms and raised them to the sky, "I am Joan of Arc, the Maid of Orleans!" he yelled in a high-pitched voice that bore no resemblance to his usual baritone, professorial tone. "I've come to Havana to proclaim love, unity and peace."

David, the photographer, surveyed his companions through his half-opened eyes. Under a palm tree, sitting on the earth, the Cosmic Brotherhood looked like the proverbial motley, discombobulated crew that it was. Maestro's skinny body was crowned by a shoulder-length mane. He wore his usual jeans and a tattered t-shirt with a fading peace sign. Maestro was twenty-eight years old but depending on his expression he could pass as a teenager, with his full lips pursed and his long eyelashes batting, or an old sage, with his toothless mouth open and his slightly bent back.

He was surrounded by his four disciples. The adults were Társila De La Vega, a short and chubby

13

spinster that channeled deceased rock stars; Paquito Pérez, a pot-smoking young man who only dealt with Ascended Masters, and David Santiesteban, a photographer of *quinceañera* parties, weddings, political events and even Santeria ceremonies. At forty-two David was the oldest guy in the group and they called him *Viejo*. His specialty was channeling Native Americans and Taíno Indians. And there was Tanya Díaz, a teenage girl who didn't channel anybody, but allowed the Cosmic Brotherhood to meet in her mother's house.

David acknowledged (if only to himself) that he wasn't a real medium like Maestro or even Társila, whose manifestations always had an authenticity seal that his lacked. He was only a creator of characters, an impersonator, but people loved his "Indians," asked them for guidance and sometimes, strange as it might sound, the answers that came out of his mouth when pretending to channel surprised David himself.

Maestro was the real thing, though. He had predicted Pope John Paul II's visit to Cuba when people still used to sneak in churches to attend Mass. He had channeled Edgar Cayce and proclaimed that American dollars would become legal in the island a week before Castro himself made the surprising announcement in Revolution Square. The reason why the spirit of the Kentucky-born clairvoyant had shown so much interest in Cuba's financial matters was still a mystery, but Don Edgardo, as they called him familiarly, was a regular ghostly guest at the Cosmic Brotherhood meetings. And to put the icing on the cake, or the strawberry on the fruit tart, Maestro was also in touch with an entity that knew in advance the winning numbers of the Venezuelan lottery and could make anybody rich, if Maestro just allowed him to do so.

The Venezuelan lottery results were announced by a Caracas radio station every Thursday morning, but due to the Cuban government's interference (gambling was prohibited in the island) it could only be heard by those who lived close enough to the sea and had radios with powerful antennas. Maestro usually learned the numbers the night before they were broadcasted but he wouldn't reveal them to anyone interested in *la lotería*. His astral contact was an unfortunate business man who had lost his earthly life in Tijuana because of unpaid gambling debts and Maestro said he feared for his disciples' safety.

There was still another reason why they worshiped Maestro—he was the only one in the group who had traveled abroad. A spiritual leader called Sri Maharishi had come in the late eighties to the little Santa Clara town where Maestro lived the life of a run-of-the-mill Cuban teenager. Sri Maharishi had figured out, or rather, had been told by ascended beings, that the young boy was a highly evolved entity, incarnated in Cuba to foster the enlightenment of its inhabitants. In the company of his mentor,

Maestro had gone to India and spent seven years at a monastery in the Himalayas. There, his guru had initiated him and passed onto him the knowledge that he would later spread among his fellow Cubans.

After his spiritual education was complete, Maestro returned to Cuba and settled in Havana to fulfill his mission, which began with the foundation of the Cosmic Brotherhood. "Jesus started his public life at thirty-three; I, ten years earlier," he would say. He carried in his wallet the picture of a long bearded guy with a serene and distant look. His disciples assumed it was Sri Maharishi.

David also had a personal reason to believe in Maestro. They had met three years before at the Masonic Grand Lodge, in Carlos III Avenue, during a lecture about the longevity secrets hidden inside the Egyptian pyramids. When the lecture ended, the two men sat in the park across the Lodge and talked about spirituality, politics, the price of cigarettes and everything else under the sun. From that day on, they got together regularly. In one of their encounters Maestro cured David of an old drinking habit. He rallied the Ascended Masters' support for his new friend, asked them to steer him away from the bottle and... voilà! Though David didn't become a teetotaler, he didn't get drunk again in the piggish, sloppy, rolling-down-in-the-gutter manner that he used to. When Maestro decided to start the Cosmic Brotherhood, David became its first member and had never regretted it.

Maestro was enveloped in an aura of mystery. For one thing, no one knew where he lived or if he had a family. He had never invited any of his followers to his house. Paquito complained that he was being hoity-toity but Tanya justified him, "I want as much as anybody else to visit Maestro," she said. "But if he were to give his address to all who asked for it, his home would be full of strangers every day. Do you think we are the only ones? He must have hundreds of disciples!"

After asking again for love and harmony, Maestro (or Joan of Arc, as he was still channeling) commanded everyone to light a candle for world peace. He stayed silent for a few minutes and when he spoke again, he did in English and in a deep, masculine voice.

"*I, too, following many and follow'd by many, inaugurate a religion, I descend into the arena... It may be I am destin'd to utter the loudest cries there, the winner's pealing shouts. Who knows? They may rise from me yet, and soar above every thing.*"

"Who's that?" Paquito whispered. "Not *la Juana*, I guess."

"It's Walt Whitman, you fool," answered Társila, also in a whisper. "He's reciting his poem *Leaves of Grass*."

"Grass," Paquito repeated, dreamily. "Did you

say grass?"

"Hush, *carajo*!"

David admired Maestro's skills to channel foreign spirits in their own language. He didn't speak English, at least not well enough to understand everything that Maestro said, but he could identify a few words. After Walt Whitman finished his recital, he delivered a speech that wasn't too different from his predecessor's—more peace, universal friendship and love, unconditional love...

David wished at times (as so did Tanya, Társila and Paquito) that the otherworldly visitors changed their tune a bit, but they didn't dare say it out loud. Maestro was known to get upset when someone expressed any ideas that reeked of disrespect. Once he had slapped Paquito for making jokes about the color of Fidel Castro's aura and the bad karma that he saw coming out of his beard. Paquito had left Tanya's house in tears.

"A guru has the right to discipline his flock," was Maestro's only comment. "We are in the world to remove darkness, including the one that dwells in our disciples' hearts."

Paquito missed several meetings, but one Wednesday evening he returned and humbly asked to be received again. Maestro welcomed him back, to everybody's contentment.

When Walt Whitman departed, Maestro lay down on the ground, exhausted. Tanya and Társila tended to him and brought him a concoction known as *jarabe de bejuco ubí*, a bitter herbal tea made with a plant that grew wild in Tanya's backyard.

Tanya's mother, Aurora—a single woman who had lost her sense of humor in a bumpy road along life— came out with four slices of stale bread and passed them around. Tanya insisted that they offer a snack to the Cosmic Brotherhood members every time they had a meeting. Her mother only agreed to keep the girl entertained at home because the Havana streets had gotten increasingly dangerous after the 1990 crisis began. But Aurora had little respect for them and much less for their leader. She called the Wednesday meetings "astral shit."

While they ate the bread and sipped the *jarabe de bejuco ubí*, abundance fell over the meeting in the curvaceous shape of Darlene Suárez, Aurora's next-door neighbor. Darlene was a long-legged brunette who made a living teaching the Kama Sutra, Cuban style, to foreign tourists. She had just had dinner with a Spaniard at La Bodeguita del Medio, a dollar-only restaurant, and brought three ham and cheese sandwiches and half a bottle of Havana Club to share with her friends. The sandwiches were divided and they all felt a certain kind of happiness that couldn't be described as spiritual.

"Full belly, happy heart," said Paquito, patting his stomach.

"This is a blessing from the ascended ones,"

declared Társila. "They knew I had only one egg left at home, and no oil to fry it."

David didn't say a word. He was too busy chomping down his portion. Even Maestro looked pleased and relaxed.

Only Tanya didn't take part in the general joy. Two months had passed since her best friend, Menina, left Havana to reunite with her mother in California. During the first weeks, Menina had written every five or six days and called several times, but there had been no news from her since early January and that made Tanya nervous. Had Menina forgotten her already?

Tanya kept having dreadful dreams in which Menina appeared covered in blood and crying for her. In the most terrifying scene, Tanya found herself in a strange apartment, with white walls like a hospital room, frantically trying to call the police so they could save her friend... She had had the same nightmare for three nights in a row, but she didn't mention it to anybody. She was happy to see Darlene, though. Her neighbor was Menina's aunt.

"Have you heard from Meni or her father?" she asked.

"No, honey," Darlene said. "My brother and I don't get along, and my sister-in-law has never written two lines to me. I'd be the last person to find out if anything were to happen."

"If anything were to happen." The phrase kept

playing in Tanya's mind for a long time, with an ominous buzzing. "If anything were to happen…" She shuddered and evoked Menina's innocent face, the sincerity in her voice when she promised, "I will never, ever forget you. We'll meet again, and sooner than you think." They had been best friends since Tanya could remember and had shared everything, from dolls to their first lipsticks to secrets about boyfriends. That is, about Menina's boyfriend, because Tanya hadn't had any yet…

Darkness filled the backyard all of a sudden, spilling over it like a river of coffee. The girl shrieked.

"*Coño*, Tanya, how jumpy you are today!" Aurora complained. "What's the matter with you?"

It was nothing unusual, just *el apagón*, the programmed blackout that took place every two nights in Centro Habana and lasted for eight or nine hours. The meeting dissolved soon. David, who lived nearby, walked to his house. Paquito and Társila went to a bus stop where they would wait for one of the massive, 18-wheel trucks called "camels" that had replaced regular buses. Maestro joined the palms and fingers of his hands and bowed.

"Namaste," he said, and took his Chinese bicycle by the handle. "See you next week."

"Isn't it dangerous to ride in the dark?" Darlene asked him. "Hey, you could spend the night with me if you want to. In a separate bed, of course," she added with a wink.

21

The Cosmic Brotherhood members suspected that Darlene had less than pure intentions. She *coveted* their guru, said Paquito, who in turn coveted Darlene. Maestro didn't look particularly appetizing because of his skinny, hairless chest and toothless smile, and the fact that he didn't have dollars put him in the negative side as a potential client. But Darlene had developed an intense interest in him after reading about the genital skills attributed to the Indian gurus. "These guys can break bricks with their *pingas*," she confided to Aurora.

"In their dreams!" Aurora replied. "I've seen pictures and they all are thin as rails. Look at Maestro! I bet he hasn't had a decent meal in years."

"I still want to try."

"Good luck."

Maestro, however, wasn't that easy to seduce.

"Thanks, but I'd rather go home," he said with his distant, illuminati expression. "I'll walk just a couple of blocks, until I reach Belascoaín Avenue. The blackout zone ends there and then I can ride safely."

"But the streets are full of potholes...," began Tanya.

"I can see in the darkness, *querida*. I learned that from Sri Maharishi."

"What about thieves and drunk drivers? Do you want to stay here, Maestro? We will give you the couch."

"I'm protected, Tanya. Stop worrying about me."

Nobody could convince him. He left, Darlene went home and Aurora wrapped up half a sandwich that she had hidden from the voracious guests.

"Come on, *niña*, let's go to bed. You have to help me clean the refrigerator the first thing in the morning."

Tanya obeyed, but she couldn't sleep. Her concern for Menina and her fears about Maestro's safety kept her awake until dawn.

If anything were to happen.

It did.

II: The little problem

Maestro lay on the bed, unconscious. His face was thinner and more emaciated than ever and his head bandaged. His eyes were closed and a tangle of tubes had been attached to his rigid body. The other Cosmic Brotherhood members surrounded him, silent and in a state of shock. David had come straight from a *quinceañera* party and looked out of place in the small, antiseptic–smelling room, with an old smoking jacket, a Nikon hanging from his right shoulder and a backpack full of lighting equipment. He still had on his shirt crumbs of a poorly made strawberry cupcake that the hostess had offered him.

A tired-looking nurse entered the room and retrieved Maestro's chart.

"Is he going to be OK?" Tanya asked, her voice as inaudible as Maestro's breathing. "Do you think he's going to be OK?"

The nurse coughed, uneasily.

"You need to ask a doctor. By the way, are any of you related to the patient?" Her eyes went from Paquito's matted hair to Társila's spinster's bun to David's bald spot to Tanya's ponytail. Since no one answered, she insisted, "Do you know if he has family? Someone has to bring in clean sheets and help give him a bath. We are understaffed and can't do everything."

"I'll bathe him," Tanya hurried to say. "And I will

bring sheets too."

David doubted that Aurora would agree to part with her bedclothes. As for him, he only had two old, stained sheets at home and there was no way to minimize his bed gear even more.

The nurse left. The Cosmic Brotherhood stayed, sharing the details they had picked up about the accident. The only thing they knew for sure was that a "camel" had hit Maestro when he rode down Belascoaín Avenue. It was difficult to understand why he hadn't noticed the presence of the vehicle, a monstrosity that puffed like an asthmatic whale, but Társila had heard that the driver was drunk out of his skull when the police arrived.

"The bastard was probably driving so fast that it didn't give Maestro time to react," she said.

"I am so sorry. I pleaded with Maestro to stay with us," Tanya repeated. "If I had insisted, maybe..."

"Stop that, *niña*. It wasn't your fault."

"I'm wondering if he can listen to us," Paquito muttered.

"He seems pretty out of it," David touched his friend's forehead. "And he's cold. Way too cold."

"But—is he still alive?"

"I think so."

Maestro breathed slightly. His bony chest moved up and down in imperceptible waves.

"He may already be in the astral plane," Tanya said.

25

The doctor—a young, stern man from the Oriente province—came in, looked around and frowned.

"Too many people, too much noise! Let's see, who is the closest relative?"

Fearing he might kick *all* of them out, David answered, "I am."

"You are his…"

"Brother."

The doctor took him by the arm and moved away from the group.

"We did an MRI this morning," he said. "He has severe brain damage and I don't think he will ever recover. You should be prepared for the worst."

* * *

Two weeks passed and the worst didn't come. Maybe thanks to the ascended beings' intervention, the many candles that the Cosmic Brotherhood lit or the endless prayers they said, Maestro started a slow journey back to recovery. The doctor was surprised to discover that he was able to mumble a few unconnected words and to get off the respirator by the fourth day, but his prognosis remained bleak. Even if Maestro survived, he stated, he would never be able to walk or to communicate—unless a miracle happened. But wasn't Maestro an expert in miracles, a miracle worker himself? His disciples kept the faith.

"He will recover soon," Tanya said confidently. "I don't know how to explain it, but I simply *feel* it."

(She felt it the same way she feared that something bad had happened to Menina.)

The Cosmic Brotherhood took turns to visit the patient. Társila, who had a part-time job as a maid for Roseta Farnós, a retired actress, brought a crocheted bedspread that her employer had donated. Aurora *did* send a sheet and a pillowcase while David and Paquito contributed with towels and bars of soap.

Maestro's blood pressure was stable and his wounds had begun to heal. The picture looked, if not rosy, at least a soothing shade of pink when it was suddenly marred by a dark spot. One evening the doctor, red-faced and pissed-off, confronted David in the hall.

"You liar! You said you were his brother and it's not true! Why did you do that, *eh?*"

David did his best to explain to explain his fib, saying that he and Maestro shared the same beliefs and that he had meant it in a religious way. The doctor, who happened to be a Santeria practitioner and was respectful of spiritual ties, calmed down.

"After Eloy's father came today and told me that his son had no brothers, I thought you guys were up to no good."

And that was how the Cosmic Brotherhood found out Maestro's real name. They didn't know he had family left in the island, either, and assumed that his parents had stayed in India with Sri Maharishi, or maybe moved to the United States. They couldn't conceive that anybody would return to Cuba after living abroad—unless he had a mission, naturally— and concluded that his guru was alone in Havana.

"Sorry about the confusion, Doc," David said.

"That's OK, bro. But be more specific next time."

David entered Maestro's room. A feeble sixty-year old mulatto was sitting by the bed, his shoulders hunched and his eyes red. As soon as he saw David, the man stood up and held out his hand.

"I'm Florencio, Eloy's dad. The nurses told me that several people have been taking care of him during the last days. Are you one of them?"

"Yes, sir."

"Thanks, *mijo*. I can't imagine how Eloy would have managed without your help... Have you known him for a long time? Are you friends?"

"I am actually one of his disciples... though I am honored to count myself among his friends as well."

Florencio looked stunned and David wished he had chosen different, simpler words. He was afraid he sounded pompous or even disingenuous. "We all care a lot about Maestro," he added. "Tanya, Társila, Paquito..."

"Who is Maestro?"

"That's how we call him."

"Wait... who do you mean by 'we'?

"His followers, sir."

"Disciples, followers... *Válgame Dios*," Florencio shrugged. "He often talked about a fraternity of some sort, but I thought it was all bullshit."

David cringed.

"I was in Pinar del Rio for the last two weeks and didn't know about the accident until last night, when I went to Eloy's room and found it empty," Florencio went on. "I was frantic."

"Do you visit him often?"

"Well, of course. He needs more or less constant supervision due to his—little problem, you know? I was afraid of leaving him alone for so many days, but I had to. My brother-in-law, who lives in Pinar del Río, had bought a pig and offered me half of it at a good price, so my daughter and I went to pick it up. All together, I have six mouths to feed. It's not easy!"

David was going to ask about "the little problem" but Florencio turned to Maestro, who had just opened his eyes.

"Eloycito, *niño*, look who is here!" he said. "Your friend… er… what's your name?"

"David."

"David came to see you"

Maestro didn't seem to recognize David or his father. After gazing at the walls for a few seconds, with a blank expression, he closed his eyes again.

"Hi, everybody!"

Tanya came in, still in her school uniform and carrying a paper bag. She nodded politely to Florencio, waved to David and approached the bed.

"What's up, Maestro?" She kissed him and took a

29

hamburger out of the bag. "Darlene sent this because the nurse says he has to start eating protein," she told David, then addressed Maestro again, "Come on, open your mouth," she took a piece of meat and pressed against his dry lips. "Take just a bite."

David touched Florencio's arm. "Why did you say Maestro...I mean, Eloy, needs constant supervision?" he whispered.

"He's sick, *mijo*. He's had mental problems for years. Didn't you guys know that?"

A chill ran through David's spine, but he recalled something Maestro had shared with them several weeks before. He had said that it was difficult for relatives to understand the responsibilities that fell upon an initiated and explained that family members tended to oppose the mission, often ridiculing the guru or spewing malicious lies about his mental health and even his morality. But he had spoken in general terms and never mentioned *his* own relatives, so David had no reason to believe he was talking from personal experience.

"Did his problem, as you called it, start after his trip to India?" he asked.

"His trip to India?"

"Yes, when he was initiated by Sri Maharishi. Because you may be confusing a spiritual experience with..."

Florencio put his hands on David's shoulders. "You don't get it," he said. "Eloy has never been to

India. He has always lived here, in Cuba. He is not initiated in anything."

They moved away from Tanya though she wasn't paying any attention to the exchange, being focused on making Maestro eat.

"He told us—," David began to say.

"Yes, I can imagine what he told you. My son is delusional. He's been under psychiatric treatment since he was a teenager."

David didn't reply. He was angry, angrier than he had felt in a long time. Hadn't Florencio been a scrawny old man he might have punched him in the face. He was ready to leave the room when Florencio said, "He's been telling you guys he has a sacred mission, hasn't he?"

David looked at the man's tear-filled eyes and a throbbing pain stabbed at his chest. It was the craving for a drink, the kind he hadn't felt during the last two years.

"Maestro founded our group, the Cosmic Brotherhood, and we have meetings every Wednesday," he said.

"The Cosmic Brotherhood… It was true, then. I came to think that he had made it up, like everything else."

"Like everything else…"

They returned to the bed.

"Maestro ate a little bit of the hamburger," Tanya said. "Then it dawned on me that he is a vegetarian!

31

Ay, what a shame! I will bring fresh fruit and some veggies next time."

David didn't answer. His faith had started to crumble like a poorly made strawberry cupcake.

III: The Venezuelan lottery

"I don't believe it!" Tanya said, indignant. "I don't believe it for one minute! His father is lying and only God knows why."

The Cosmic Brotherhood had met under the palm tree to discuss Maestro's hoax, as Aurora called it.

"Didn't I always say the guy was cuckoo?" she asked with the irritating grin of a skeptic proved right. "His 'manifestations' and all this channeling stuff are a ton of astral crap," she glared at David, who pretended not to notice. "What a bunch of con artists!"

"Mom, Maestro is not a con artist!" Tanya protested. "In any case, he is... what did his father say? De... illusional."

"Delusional, my ass! Nuts who don't get lost ain't nuts. He was just putting on a show to kill time and eat *for free* in my house."

"You only gave him a slice of stale bread and a glass of b*ejuco ubí* tea. What a feast!"

"Feast or no feast, he gulped everything down. What did he want, roast beef for supper? *No me jodas*!"

Aurora stalked off. Her best friend, a bespectacled lady that Tanya called *Tía* Lourdes, was in the living room and soon the women's chuckles could be heard in the backyard.

"Remember his prophecies," Tanya said. "He was

33

right about the Pope's coming and the legalization of the dollar, wasn't he?"

For the first time David thought that both events might not have been too hard to guess. Dollars had been circulating in the Cuban underground economy for years but their trade was out of the government's hands. The only way the state had to control the American currency's flow was making it legal. As for the Pope's visit, John Paul II had trotted all over the world. He had traveled to several communist countries before; it wasn't so surprising that he finally included Cuba in his itinerary.

"And the lottery," Társila added. "He knew the winning numbers before anyone else."

"But he never announced them until the following morning," Paquito replied. "When *some* people already knew."

"He waited because he didn't want us to gamble."

"He said it wasn't right to use his *saddhis*, his spiritual powers, for personal gain."

"Nonsense," Paquito shrugged. "You girls don't want to face the truth. The guy is crazy! His old man has no reason to lie to us."

"Shut up!"

"Remember the day he slapped me because I made an innocent joke? I don't know about you, but *I* haven't forgotten."

Even Tanya kept quiet after that.

"I think we should wait until he recovers," David

said at last. "It's not fair to discuss all this and make assumptions without giving Maestro a chance to defend himself."

"That's right!" Tanya's eyes lit. "You are a true friend, *Viejo*."

Aurora came back bringing the usual slices of bread and four cups of *bejuco ubí* tea.

"Nuts who don't get lost ain't nuts," she repeated. "He didn't want to be found out, that's why he didn't say where he lived or introduce you to his family. Your 'guru' is a fake, admit it."

"The same was said about Jesus until he resurrected," Társila grumbled.

"Now we have a second Messiah, Saint Eloy of Havana. And you guys are Eloyians, apostles of the Astral Sect of the Shit Eaters! Ha!"

"Please, don't pay any attention to her." Tanya whispered, blushing. "She is an untrained, green soul."

"Should we continue helping him out?" Paquito asked.

"Yes," Tanya said firmly. "He is still our guru, even if he lied a bit. And that hasn't been proved yet."

In any case, didn't they need the lies? David wondered as he walked back to his house. The evenings they spent with the spirits, under Maestro's guidance, were the only solace they all had. They couldn't afford to go to dollar-only restaurants and the few cafeterias where food was sold in pesos were constantly packed out. They couldn't travel to the beaches because "camels" passed every three or four hours, crammed to the maximum capacity. Prices in the dollar-only shops called *diplotiendas* were also well beyond their means. The two TV channels repeated over and over the same programs— movies that had been hits thirty years before, dull documentaries and political harangues...

Was it wrong that Maestro tried to free them from their permanent boredom, at least for a few hours a week? Was it wrong to entertain visitors like Walt Whitman, Edgar Cayce and Joan of Arc... or his own, counterfeit Native Americans? All in all, it had been fun.

And yet—David remembered the times he had pretended to channel an Apache warrior or a Navajo shaman. He had always felt guilty, the only phony in a pious assembly, but now it turned out that Maestro had been faking it too. And probably Társila as well, and that dopey Paquito... Except for Tanya, who had never claimed to experience a manifestation or channeled anybody, they all had lied shamelessly. Fun or no fun, Aurora was right—they had been eating astral crap and the moment had come to regurgitate it.

David stopped in front of El Bar Cincuentenario. A sign written on a dirty cardboard read *Doubles, three pesos*. He hesitated for a moment, then called to the bartender, "Give me two doubles, man."

After Maestro spent a month in the hospital, the doctor found him ready to be discharged. He was able to swallow on his own and to say a few words. But there was no way that his brain could recover totally and he would always need around-the-clock care. He also needed an adjustable bed, which the hospital management couldn't provide. Fortunately, David knew a widow who happened to be selling one for forty dollars. With Darlene's help (she contributed thirty one), the Cosmic Brotherhood purchased it. The next question was where to take it.

Florencio shared a one-bedroom apartment with his daughter Nena, who was a single mother, and her three little girls. Nena said in no uncertain terms that they didn't have the space or the proper conditions to accommodate a sick man there.

"Where are we going to put his bed, in the bathroom?" she snapped. "He'd be better off in his own place and we will keep an eye on him."

As a disabled person who officially lived by himself, Maestro had the right to receive public health assistance. The hospital would send a nurse to check on him once a week.

"Nena is right," Florencio said. "It wouldn't be safe to move Eloy to our apartment, with all the kids running around. Let's keep him in his room and I'll come by every day and bring him food."

"What a cold-hearted family!" Tanya told David. "They don't care about Maestro, period. See why I don't believe a word of what they say?"

The Cosmic Brotherhood helped Florencio transport Maestro to his home, a room located in a rundown Malecón Drive tenement house. Tanya, who was the first one to get there, looked at the closed door with reverence, wishing she could sneak inside before the others arrived. Then she saw a neighbor, a chunky woman who crossed the yard with a bucket of water in one hand and a towel in the other. Tanya couldn't help sharing the news with her.

"Maestro... I mean, Eloy, will be back today!" she said.

The woman shrugged. "*El loquito*? Yes, I heard he was locked up."

"He was *in the hospital*," Tanya corrected her. "After a traffic accident, you know?"

"Whatever."

The woman stepped inside the communal bathroom, which was surrounded by a swarm of flies, and hung the towel over the door.

"And he is not crazy!" Tanya yelled, though it was now too late. "I don't care what you guys say, he isn't!"

An ambulance stopped in front of the tenement. Florencio came out and opened the room.

"Do you want to come in, girl?" he asked.

Tanya followed him, shaking slightly. It was a single room with just one window, and it smelled of mold, dirt and old papers. The walls were lined up with handmade shelves full of books about spirituality and metaphysics (Tanya had borrowed some of them) and a rusty Primus stove occupied a corner. Everything had the slippery feel of decaying matter.

A Chinese folding screen marked the separation between the sleeping area (where the adjustable bed would replace a stained military cot) and what Tanya assumed was a meditation space. A full-sized portrait of a long-haired, fiery-eyed man had been propped against a wooden box and there were five votive candles scattered in front of it. The picture looked like the one that Maestro kept in his wallet.

"Sri Maharishi?" Tanya whispered.

"Hey, girl! Can you lend us a hand here?" David yelled.

She ran outside.

"My wife used to take good care of Eloy," Florencio explained, after Maestro was comfortably settled in his new bed. "She would come every day, cook for him, clean his room... After she passed away I've tried to do the same, but with three grandkids at home I can't do much. Thank God Eloy has become more responsible but sometimes he simply forgets to eat."

Tanya, who was sweeping the floor, turned to him, "That won't happen again, Florencio. We won't let him forget, I promise."

"Bless your heart."

Over cups of watery coffee, Maestro's life was
finally puzzled together in front his followers' eyes.
Tanya listened silently, trying to conciliate it with
the stories that her guru had shared at the Cosmic
Brotherhood meetings. He hadn't finished high school
due to a learning disability, his father said, but he
would read every book he could get his hands on. He
had been interned (actually, Florencio said "locked
up") in Mazorra Psychiatric Hospital for months at a
time and given electroshock treatments. And definitely,
the old man could attest to that, his son had never,
ever travelled out of Cuba.

"He doesn't even have a passport, as far as I
know," Florencio said.

Tanya's heart sank, but then she had a revelation,
the closest thing to a manifestation that she had ever
felt. What if Maestro had gone to India in his astral
body? He hadn't talked about requesting an exit visa
or asking for the government's permission to leave the
island, which were the regular procedures for anybody
who wanted to go abroad. But why would he bother
with the Cuban red tape when his *siddhis* allowed him
to move in a safer, easier way?

"This room belonged to my father and he left
it to Eloy before passing away," Florencio went on.
"We were so happy that he finally had his own space.
Sometimes sharing a house with him was—difficult.
Once he took the refrigerator door off its hinges and
threw it out the window."

"Did he have any girlfriends?" David asked.

"He once lived with an older lady for a couple of months, but the arrangement didn't work out. I don't think that he could—you know, perform, with so much medication and stuff."

Tanya frowned. Wasn't that too much information? The Cosmic Brotherhood members didn't need to know that, did they?

A routine was soon established. The Cosmic Brotherhood worked in shifts during the day, feeding Maestro and keeping his room tidy while Florencio or Nena came every evening to spend the night with him. The only thing that troubled Tanya was Maestro's refusal to eat on his own. He could do it, the doctor said, but he simply didn't want to. The reason for his stubbornness could be traced back to the few, unintelligible words he muttered from time to time.

"The astral... plane. I am... in the astral plane."

If Maestro thought he was in another dimension, Tanya figured out, there was no need for him to eat. She had once asked him what he thought about the Catholic concepts of purgatory, heaven and hell. "They don't exist," Maestro had answered. "We all go to the same place, the astral plane, where we are met by our guru or by old, trusted friends and relatives. There we stay for a while—until we are ready to reincarnate."

"What's the astral plane like?"

"It's a no-time and no-space zone, a void where

souls feel no carnal desires, no appetite, nothing… After reviewing their lives, they simply float around and wait. There is no punishment or reward there. That is left for the next life, when they reap whatever they sowed."

With that in mind, Tanya made another attempt to reach out to him.

"You are not in the astral plane, Maestro," she whispered in his ear. "This is Havana, Cuba. You are at home."

"Home."

"Here, taste this guava *pastelito*."

She always kept a generous supply of sweets provided by Darlene, who said that, if Maestro was in fact a con artist, his trickery tipped scales in his favor. "Men shouldn't be *too* holy," she said, laughing. "Nice guys finish last, don't they?"

Usually Maestro didn't recognize anyone, but the day of the *pastelito* he fixed his dilated pupils on Tanya and struggled to touch her hand.

"You look like someone I used to know," he muttered, the first coherent sentence he had pronounced since the accident. "Are you dead too?"

Tanya was so thrilled to hear him talk that she forgot to answer his question.

"Maestro, you are back! I knew the silly doctor was all wrong! How are you feeling?"

That turned out to be a short-lived spark—Maestro closed his eyes again and went to sleep for the rest of the day—but the girl was ecstatic.

"He can talk and he can think," she informed the Cosmic Brotherhood. "He's going to make it, guys!"

"You know what?" Florencio said to the spiritual team, upon finding them congregated in Maestro's room. "It may be… it just may be that there is some truth in all this mystical stuff he loved to talk about."

Like a freshly watered plant, the disciples' faith revived. Tanya, though she hadn't yet gotten news from Menina, felt optimistic. Maestro would recover, of course, and he would help her find out what was going on with her friend. "Next time he talks to me, I will ask him if Menina is… in the astral plane as well. It may so happen that he can come in and out of the no-time and no-space zone."

One Saturday morning, it was Tanya's turn to go to Maestro's room to change his sheets and wash him. At first she had felt uncomfortable seeing the man's limp, nude body, but she had gotten used to it and now took care of him with the serene expertise of a nurse. That day Maestro seemed more out of it than ever and the girl looked for ways to cheer him up.

"We are going to listen to music, Maestro," Tanya said, because she made a point of addressing him as if he were able to understand everything. "I hope we can find salsa, chaquiti-boom-boom-boom! Unless you prefer classical stuff…Let's see what we have here."

She turned on the radio but couldn't recognize

the station. The announcer was talking about a demonstration that had just taken place in front of the government's offices and someone (a guest in the program, it seemed) said in an angry voice, "We're tired of having communism crammed down our throats!"

Scared, Tanya turned down the volume. It took her a while to understand that the program was broadcasted from Caracas. She kept listening for a good half hour, laughing at the critical comments about Hugo Chavez, but when the anchor said it was time to announce the previous night's lottery winners, the girl's face fell and she turned off the radio. She didn't a say a word about it, though.

IV: Mise-en-scène

"What am I doing here? Where have the Ascended Masters gone? What are you doing to me? Who are you?"

These were the questions Maestro repeated whenever he spoke. He pronounced them more clearly every day and his voice was stronger. His hearing was not damaged either; he jumped up at unexpected noises and got anxious when the next-door neighbors started a fight. He could hear the explanations that his friends gave him, but somehow they didn't reach his brain, or the mysterious place where his intelligence resided.

"The camel hit me... I felt the impact, saw the light at the end of the tunnel, followed it—Now, I'm in the fourth dimension. Or am I not?"

"No, Maestro, you are at home," Tanya answered. "You had an accident, yes, but you survived. Look at me."

"Is this part of the *lila*, the divine play?"

"Maestro..."

"He's convinced that he died in the accident," David said. "He thinks he must be... out there, somewhere in the astral plane."

"But can't he see us? Listen to us?"

"You know that his mind is..."

They kept him fed through the IV, but his body began to grow lighter and his bones more fragile. He developed sores on his back and calves despite the massages that Tanya administered every time she bathed him. The nurse who came to check on him once a week said that he needed to start eating on his own and moving, even if for only a few minutes a day.

"He can't stay like this indefinitely," she warned Florencio. "He is losing weight despite the IV, and time is running out."

The Cosmic Brotherhood met in Tanya's house for a special session. Though they prayed and meditated individually they hadn't, as a group, been in contact with the spirits after the accident. Only Paquito had tried once, but in vain—the Ascended Masters didn't pay any attention to his incoherent blabbering.

That evening, right before the meeting, they lit a candle and said a special prayer though nobody attempted to channel. They were in a good mood, particularly David, who had stopped by El Bar Cincuentenario on his way and felt almost divinely guided after three shots of rum.

"We need to find a way to bring Maestro back," Tanya said. "If not, we are going to lose him."

"He just has to understand that he's alive," Paquito said. "It shouldn't be too difficult."

"But how do we explain it to him? I've tried so many times…"

"He seems to look *through* us," Társila said. "Like he is seeing me, but doesn't recognize me as Társila."

"He refuses to eat and won't even touch my *pasteles*," Tanya shook her head. "I can lift him so easily now… he must be weighing less than ninety pounds."

An idea started to form in David's alcohol-infused brain. The thought approached him slowly, almost tentatively, like a scaredy cat. He kept quiet until the idea took shape, while the others talked among themselves. Once he had grabbed it by its fluffy, furry tail, he spoke, trying not to slur his words, "We have to meet him in the astral plane. That's where he thinks he is and that's where we have to go."

"But he *isn't* in the astral plane, you fool!"

"Then we have to send him there."

Everybody stared at him in horror.

"Killing Maestro, you mean?"

"You are out of your mind, *borracho*!"

David was not offended because they called him a drunk. He waited for the storm of insults to end and went on, "You didn't let me finish, dimwits. I didn't mean that literally. What I was trying to say, when I was so rudely interrupted, was that we should make him *believe* he is in the astral plane. Then we can order him to return to earth and resume his mission."

"How are we going to do that?"

"By playing a trick."

"What kind of trick?"

"Now, listen…"

* * *

David's plan sounded easy to carry out, at least in its preliminary stages. They would set up the scene, so as to speak, and pretend that Sri Maharishi was there, having a spiritual encounter with his disciple. He would command Maestro to eat and walk and assure him that he wasn't dead. Sri Maharishi would be played by David, conveniently disguised.

"Walt Whitman must show up too," Paquito said. "It was the last spirit Maestro channeled and one of his favorites. He will have a good influence on him."

"But I don't speak English and you don't either. Old Walt always spoke in his own language."

Tanya volunteered to borrow a recording of *Leaves of Grass* from her English teacher. "We can play it in the background, to remind him of Walt."

"What about Joan of Arc?" Társila asked.

"I don't have any French recordings."

"It doesn't matter. She addressed us in plain Spanish. What if she just—makes a cameo? She doesn't need to say a word, just be present as a supportive figure."

"*Qué* cameo *ni* cameo!" David protested. "How is she going to show up?"

It turned out that Társila wanted to use some histrionic skills that nobody knew she possessed.

"I can play Joan's role."

"You are taking this to extremes!"

"*Ay*, David, don't be jealous. We are simply enhancing your original idea."

"Yes, expanding on it."

By majority vote, Joan of Arc stayed. They moved on to another topic and appointed Paquito as the special effects technician. His duty was to make sure that the recording started on time and to dim the lights at the right moment.

"We should turn all the lights off and get a bunch of candles instead," Társila said. "Candles are more spiritual."

"Don't go around playing with fire," Aurora barged in. "I know what's going to happen. You will burn down his room and then want to bring the lazy bum here. And I am not going to allow it!"

Tanya lowered her head. She had actually thought about offering shelter to Maestro.

Paquito put Aurora at ease. They wouldn't use candles, but a set of clear Christmas lights that Darlene had bought last December. They flashed and produced quite a ghostly, otherworldly effect.

Before leaving, the Cosmic Brotherhood agreed to have a rehearsal. It would take place that very weekend because time, as the nurse had said, was running out.

It rained all morning on Saturday, but the weather didn't deter the Cosmic Brotherhood members. Their collective energy had returned and they felt like in the good old days when Maestro had led them. David didn't even pass by El Bar Cincuentenario, too busy reading about Sri Maharishi and looking for the most appropriate way to impersonate him. Tanya borrowed the cassette with Walt Whitman's poems and a tape recorder from his English teacher and Paquito built a wood frame for the Christmas lights.

Társila brought an outfit taken from a Victorian play in which Roseta Farnós had had a leading role twenty years before. She locked herself in Aurora's room and came out in full costume, wearing a purple dress with an attached crinoline and a fake-pearl choker. A colossal blonde wig added three inches to her height.

"But Joan of Arc was a warrior!" David said. "Shouldn't you wear a suit of armor instead? This dress is an anachronism."

"Roseta didn't have any suits of armor," Társila replied. "I will be playing Joan *before* she went to war."

"She was a peasant girl, not a duchess. And petticoats were not invented yet."

"*Viejo*, cut it out! This is only to create... ambiance. I didn't know you were so picky!"

Társila had also borrowed from Roseta a voice changer for David, in case Maestro wanted to talk to Sri Maharishi. "I am just trying to help and all you do is criticize me!" she whined.

David apologized.

Walt Whitman's poems, read by a Jamaican actor with a thick accent, had a couple of glitches in "I met a seer, passing the hues and objects of the world," but there was no time to find a different one.

"First, Sri Maharishi will appear and deliver his speech," said Társila, who had appointed herself as the scene director. "You need a wig too, David, because your hair is too short... But don't worry, Roseta has dozens of them. You will say to Maestro, 'My dear son, come forth!' The lights will start flashing and we will hear *Leaves of Grass* softly in the background. Next, *I* will come in, caress his cheeks and say with a French accent, 'You arre fine, Maestrro...Go back and rresume yourr teaching,' and I will keep walking around for a while. And to close the session... more music! Here is a cassette of sacred Tibetan chants. How is that?"

David thought they had gone too far and was tempted to call the whole thing off, but after seeing everybody in action he felt surprisingly satisfied. For an amateur crew like that, the staging wasn't bad, he admitted. It wasn't bad at all.

Only Aurora, who had watched the rehearsal in suspicious silence, cracked up, "The guy is going to open his eyes, take a good look at you and die of laughter!"

The performance was scheduled for a Wednesday evening. Florencio had to take Maestro to the hospital in the morning and that would give the Cosmic Brotherhood members a chance to prepare the room in his absence. They had decided not to inform the old man of their plans. The shadow of mystifications that enveloped them could hurt his paternal feelings or worse, make him even more distrustful of his son's spiritual powers.

Setting the stage was simple. Tanya polished the glass that covered Sri Maharishi's photo. David (who looked more or less like the India-born guru with a brown wig and a white tunic) would crouch behind until it was his time to make a formal entrance. The set of Christmas lights, attached to a frame that resembled a human body ("sort of an aura," Tanya said) was placed next to the picture. At the right moment, Paquito would turn on the lights and David would stand under the flashing bulbs. It would seem as if the guru himself had leaped off his picture.

"Like in that A-ha song, *Take on me*, remember?" said Tanya. "Menina used to sing it all the time. *Oh, the things that you say... is it life or just a play? I'll be coming for you anyway.*"

Thinking of her friend saddened Tanya again. There hadn't been any news yet, or if there were, no one was telling her. A few days before Darlene had come to visit and had a long, whispering conversation with Aurora. Afterwards, both women had started to cry. Had they been talking of Menina? Tanya didn't dare to ask. Her only hope was Maestro, who always had an answer for her...

The tape recorder and the cassettes with

Whitman's poems and the Hindu music were ready. As for Joan of Arc, David had managed to convince Társila to be only a silent presence.

"That's what a 'cameo' means, right?"

"But Maestro needs to know that I am Joan. How will he find out if I don't say so?" she protested.

"Don't worry, Tarsilita, he will know who you are," replied David, still inspired despite his sobriety. "You already convey her luminous spirit in a *magnificent* manner."

"Well, that is true."

At five p.m. Florencio and his son returned from the hospital. The old man, exhausted after a day spent carrying Maestro around, was happy to abandon him to his disciples' hands.

"You guys are my heroes," he said.

David silently wished they could prove him right.

"And thanks for rearranging his room. It looks much better now."

"No problem, Florencio," Tanya said. "We did it with great pleasure. What did the doctor say?"

"He was a little more hopeful than the last time. He told me that, save for the sores and the general weakness, Eloy isn't in too bad a shape, but we still need to make him eat solid food as soon as possible."

"We will."

Tanya looked around but there was no food left in the room. She was sorry, not only because they would waste a great opportunity to entice Maestro to eat, if the trick worked out, but because she herself was awfully hungry. She hadn't eaten anything since breakfast and her stomach was growling in the most unspiritual way. At any rate, she still had one dollar that Darlene had given to her. *I can run to a diplotienda and bring back a couple of bananas, if he says that he wants to eat,* she thought.

When Florencio left, they gave the final touches to the scene. The Christmas lights were placed to the right of Sri Maharishi's picture. Társila hid behind the folding screen and got into her petticoats after ordering the men to turn their backs to her.

"Don't look until I say I'm done, eh!!"

Maestro opened his eyes around seven p.m., when the last rays of sun were gone and the entire room was in twilight. He looked around and asked, "Is... anyone... here?" He seemed surprised to find himself alone—there was always someone with him, day and night.

Tanya and Társila waited behind the folding screen. They were sitting on the floor and it was hard and cold. Tanya remembered how uncomfortable it was also to sit under the palm tree, with ants getting under her clothes, biting her flesh, and small rocks hurting her legs. She wondered if she would ever get to experience enlightenment in a nice, comfy place.

David, hidden behind Sri Maharishi's picture,

reflected on Maestro's words. *He knows when we are around, then. He just pretends he doesn't. We believe we are bullshitting him and may end up on the receiving end of this self-actualized crap.*

But now it was too late to stop. At Paquito's prompt, he adjusted the voice changer and said in his most tender, love-and-wisdom-filled tone, "Peace be with you, Eloy, my beloved disciple. Peace be with you."

Maestro lifted his head. He did it without help, for the first time. David came out. The Christmas lights started to flash and surrounded him with a glowing halo.

"Sri Maharishi," Maestro muttered. "I've been waiting for you... I am ready to review this life and lift the veil of *maya*."

"No, Eloy," David replied. "We aren't lifting any veils yet. It is not your time, my son. I simply came to tell you that you are still earthbound. You founded the Cosmic Brotherhood and you have to take it to its final, glorious stage. You can't just give up now."

"What do you mean?" Maestro's voice was clear, with no trace of weakness or confusion. "I am dead! I'm in the first stage of *bardo*."

"No, *señor*! I mean, you aren't ready to transcend yet. I command you to eat, drink and—live! The ascended beings and your guardian angels, as well as all the evolved spirits who dwell in higher dimensions, have the same message for you."

Paquito hit the play button and the Jamaican poet began his recital, but Maestro paid no attention to it.

"Sri Maharishi, why do you call me Eloy?"

David, who hadn't counted on the ad lib situation, was caught off guard. He had chosen to use Maestro's real name because he assumed that Sri Maharishi wouldn't call his disciple "master."

"Well... because it is your name, my son."

"But that is not the one you gave me at my initiation."

"I am using it ... er... I am using it to remind you of your earthly obligations."

"But Baba... you look different now. You are much shorter than when I met you. And you speak with a Cuban accent, which you didn't use to."

David's face got red and he felt the familiar rush of anger running through his body. *The little bastard knows perfectly well that this is a comedy. He's just pulling my leg!*

The recording stopped. It was Társila's turn to enter the scene, but she didn't appear. David walked to the folding screen and shook it. "Are you coming out or what?" he hissed.

There was no answer.

She knows, too. Well, that's the end. The hell with it.

David turned off the voice changer.

"Come on, Maestro," he said. "The game is over."

The Christmas lights went out. David thought

that Paquito had also gotten tired of playing "special effects technician," but then he heard the next-door neighbor's screams through the paper-thin wall.

"The blackout again, *mierda*! We weren't supposed to have one tonight, were we?"

Társila and Tanya stumbled in the darkness toward David.

"It's *el apagón*," Tanya whispered. "What are we going to do?"

"Just have an honest conversation with Maestro... or Eloy," David replied.

"What if he gets mad?"

"In any case, *we* are the ones who should be mad at him," David said, not caring if Maestro heard him or not; in fact, secretly wanting him to hear his complaints. "Don't you see he's been playing fucking mind games with us?"

"But what is Paquito doing now?" asked Társila.

A tenuous luminosity had started to enfold the room.

"He must have kept a candle for special effects."

"That's not a candle, David! Look, look at Maestro!"

"No, it... can't be."

"It is."

* * *

Maestro, wrapped up in a golden aura, floated five inches above the bed. Paquito, the tape recorder at his feet, gaped at him, his mouth opened and both hands stretched toward the hovering figure.

"Oh, you all are here," Maestro pierced them with his immense, bright eyes. "I am so happy to see you again, even if it is the last time."

"But you are not leaving now, Maestro, are you?" only Tanya could have asked that.

"I am not sure, *querida*. I have received contradictory messages," Maestro glided and got closer to them. The girl winked because the light that surrounded the guru was now blinding.

"At first, it seemed that Sri Maharishi ordered me to go back, but then he disappeared and everything got dark. And now..."

Tanya realized that the floor had turned soft and warm, like a goose down comforter. The luminosity that emanated from Maestro had expanded, filling the room and changing it in the process. The bed and the folding screen whirled and vanished and so did the walls, the Christmas lights and even Sri Maharishi's picture. They were in a vast, wall-less, infinite space where trays full of fresh fruit drifted around, like glass boats floating in an invisible sea. The trays were made of a transparent, almost liquid material and apples, strawberries, grapes and bananas also appeared to be floating, swathed in the golden light that lit the entire place.

"So this is the astral plane," David said.

"I am not sure," Maestro repeated. "This looks

more like… a kind of in-between dimension. No man's land in Soulworld."

"No man's land feels good," Tanya said, grabbing an apple.

David looked at Társila and Paquito. Both were busy having their first taste of grapes and strawberries.

"What will happen when the lights come back?" he asked, not addressing anybody in particular.

"I don't think there are lights here," Maestro replied. "Or blackouts, for that matter."

"That's phenomenal… what else can we eat?" asked Paquito, cleaning his chin. "I'm ashamed to admit I have the munchies. I need something more solid than fruit. Something like protein, you know?"

"What about chicken pot pie?" Menina said and all heads, including Maestro's, turned to her.

The girl had come out of nowhere. She looked slightly plumper than the last time they had seen her and wore a pink blouse and jeans. There were dark shadows under her eyes and a scar crossed her throat, but she was still the same old happy, sweet-tempered Menina. She approached them, marching fast through the vastness and carrying a covered dish.

"You won't believe it, Tanya," she said, "but I made this pie all by myself!"

Menina placed the dish on the air, next to the fruit trays, and it stood in perfect balance for an everlasting instant.

Menina and the *Chupacabras*

I: Starting to forget

The plane began its descent and the clouds parted, offering Menina her first glimpse of California's face. The San Diego landscape emerged among white cotton patches like a kaleidoscopic postcard. Menina pressed her nose against the window and looked at the caravan of miniature cars that filled the roads below. But her mind still had vivid images of the cracked Havana streets and the slogans painted on murals and walls (*With Fidel until 2020! Socialism or Death*). She thought she could see again the Malecón seawall and inhale the sweet and sour smell that rose from the ocean…

"Are you tired?" her father asked. Menina shook her head and her brown ponytail hit Pablo's shoulder. "We are almost there. This is America, girl!"

Menina had never seen her father so cheerful but if someone looked tired, it was him. She wanted to smooth the fine lines that branded his forehead as she had ironed his shirts and handkerchiefs during the last four years.

"Your mother will be shocked to see how tall you are. She left you when you were a little girl and now you are ready to have a *quinceañera* party," He smiled

60

and closed his eyes, resting his head on the seat.

Menina picked up just one phrase—*she left you*—
and it began to gyrate inside her head, drilling down
to her heart until it nestled there. Luisa, her paternal
grandmother, had repeated it a hundred times, "Your
mother left you. She dumped you as if you were a
rotten potato. *Qué cochina*, what a selfish broad!"

Ana, Menina's mother, had left Cuba on a raft
in 1994. After a revolt in the Havana streets the
government "opened up the Malecón," as people said.
Those who wanted to leave the island in rubber inner
tubes, handmade boats and rafts were allowed to go.
No passports or visas were needed, no exit permits, no
tickets… Ana, who used to attend the meetings called
by the Committee for the Defense of the Revolution
wearing green fatigues and had once painted a street
mural to honor the Army Forces, shed her *miliciana*
disguise and set her eyes on the Miami shores. "It's
now or never, Pablo. If we miss this chance, we'd have
to stay here for the rest of our lives. And things are
getting worse by the day."

Pablo agreed but his mother, a stanch communist,
refused to follow them. Tensions mounted. Ana, Pablo
and their next-door neighbors collected the materials
and built a frail raft in two weeks while Luisa walked
around calling them worms and traitors. Menina,
who had just turned ten years old, was scared and
confused. Nobody bothered to explain to her what was
going on and the girl often woke up at night feeling

an unexplainable weight on her chest that dragged her down.

At the last minute, under his mother's prodding, Pablo backed off. "I am not going to risk my daughter's life in that bathtub," he said, his pale hands shaking. "Things will change, eventually. Let's wait."

"*Pendejo*!" his wife yelled. "Stay and kiss Fidel's beard if you want, but *I*'m out of here!'"

Luisa threw her daughter-in-law out of the house. She hurled a couple of dresses, a pair of shoes and a ragged blouse to the street and Ana hurled them back. "Stick them up your big fat ass, old woman. I won't need them in Miami!"

"You'll end up in a shark's belly!"

"You wish!"

The entire neighborhood rejoiced in the fight. Menina stood at the threshold, holding her father's hand until the raft disappeared in the distance like a sick animal carried on the *balseros*' shoulders.

Ana and her fellow rafters made it to Miami. A few weeks later an agreement was reached between the Cuban and the American governments and Castro "closed" the Malecón again.

In the meantime, and much to their surprise, Menina, Pablo and Luisa were praised as model communists. Teachers used the girl as an example of loyalty to the revolution, a little patriot who had chosen her homeland over a dishonorable mother.

They placed her in the first row during the protest marches in front of the American Interest Section in Havana. The school principal gave her a Cuban flag, a copper medal, a red beret and a Che Guevara T-shirt. Some kids felt sorry for her while others envied the week of fame she enjoyed. But Tanya, her best friend, thought she had been a fool.

"Why did you stay?" she asked, pinching Menina's arm. "You had an opportunity to go to *La Yuma* and you missed it. Don't you know life is awesome there? Haven't you seen any movies, eh?"

"But what could I do?" Menina protested. "My *Papi* didn't want to leave…"

"Then your *Papi* is a fool too."

Menina's world was changed forever. Pablo, who had always been introverted, became even more silent and withdrawn. He started praying to an old Sacred Heart print that Luisa kept hidden in the kitchen. Words like "leaving," "staying," "homeland" and "America" lost their first, simpler meaning. They became symbols of betrayal, indifference, resistance and loss.

Ana lived in Miami for a year and then moved to San Diego "in search of better opportunities," as she wrote to her husband. (They had had an epistolary reconciliation of some sort.) Menina thought that her mother had become rich, if not a millionaire, because every month she would send money and packages with clothes, toys and food. She became a distant, fairy godmother whose magic wand was made of American dollar bills. Distance, however, took its toll. Menina began to call Luisa *Mamá* and no one objected to that.

But two years later Luisa died after a memorable fight with her youngest daughter, Darlene *La Jinetera*. Darlene was a hooker, though she dealt *only* with foreigners, as she was quick to point out. She had a tall and handsome Cuban boyfriend, Miguel Angel, an engineer who worked as a waiter in a clandestine restaurant called Paladar Cuba Libre. They loved each other, Darlene explained to Menina. She and Miguel Angel would get married someday, in that remote but perfect future when "things" finally changed... Or she might find a filthy rich foreigner who would take her abroad with him. Once in another country, she'd dump the sucker and send for Miguel Angel. For the time being, he allowed her to work in the streets and to dance every night at the Café Havana nightclub and she never cheated on him with any Cuban man.

Luisa had forbidden Menina to visit Darlene, even to talk to her. "I don't want you to hang out with that *putona*!" she said. Pablo scowled when his sister phoned them and, in the end, blamed Darlene for their mother's death. Menina, who had always adored her young and perky aunt, didn't understand it. Darlene had procured the expensive foreign drugs that alleviated Luisa's stomach pain and brought whole chickens so they could make *caldo de pollo*. Why was her *jinetera* job such a big deal?

After his mother's death Pablo sank into a depression. The circumstances didn't help—the former Soviet Union, now dismembered, had stopped sending oil and canned food to Cuba; the crisis, euphemistically called "special period," worsened. Menina lost ten pounds and Pablo's eyesight began deteriorating due to polyneuritis, a vitamin deficiency. Discouraged, he accepted Ana's offer to meet again in the United States. She would pay for their tickets, visas and all travel expenses. The only thing he would need to do, his wife explained over the phone, was to take a plane to Miami, bringing Menina with him.

That morning, a year and a mountain of paperwork later, Menina and Pablo had finally arrived in Miami. Ana couldn't meet them ("It makes no sense for me to buy another ticket and be there only a couple of hours," she had said. "You just have to change planes.") After leaving Customs, they decided to stay inside the airport and wait for the San Diego flight. They didn't have any close friends in Miami and were afraid of getting lost in a strange city, so they wandered around, killing time for three hours. They peeked inside the duty-free stores, struggled to wash their hands in the mystifying restrooms' sinks and stood open-mouthed in front of *La Carreta*, a cafeteria that offered traditional Cuban dishes. Menina watched in awe. *Alabao*, those chicken-fried steaks, the huge ham-and-cheese sandwiches and the jumbo shrimps wrapped in red sauce...

Ana had sent them fifty dollars for travel emergencies and Pablo ordered two Cuban sandwiches, two Coca Colas, a flan and a piece of chocolate cake, but Menina wasn't able to eat more than a few bites. The knot in her throat was as tight as Aunt Darlene's working clothes. Besides, Maestro (the only member of the Cosmic Brotherhood who had traveled outside Cuba) had advised her to be careful and not to eat too much during the first days, because her stomach could get "frightened" with excessive food...

The plane shook slightly and Pablo woke up with a jolt. He looked around as if he had forgotten what they were doing there.

"Are you okay, sweetheart?" he asked after a while.

"Sure, *Papi*. Go back to sleep."

"I'd better stay awake, *hija*. We will be landing soon."

Menina clutched nervously the blue vinyl purse where she had her most prized possession. It was a snapshot of Tanya and Maestro, the Cosmic Brotherhood leader, standing under a palm tree in Tanya's backyard.

"Come to visit me soon, Maestro," she whispered, and blinked away the tears that swelled up in her eyes.

But when a voice announced in English the time and weather conditions in San Diego, the girl suddenly felt that Havana, Tanya and Maestro were a million miles away. Even Camilo, the boyfriend who had dumped her, the guy she couldn't stop thinking about until her last day in the island, had vanished from her thoughts. The closer the plane got to the runway, the more blurred Menina's memories became, like old black-and-white pictures. She was amazed at how fast she had started to forget.

The girl made an effort to conjure her mother's image. Ana was tall and thin, with a high-pitched voice and a short temper. During her last months in Havana she and Pablo had fought constantly; she would accuse him of being too passive and unable to fight for the *fulas*, the American dollars that circulated in the underground economy. Luisa defended her son and Pablo stood in the middle, as silent as the Sacred Heart print, but less forceful-looking than the serious and bearded Christ.

Everybody fought for the *fulas*. Darlene got them from her clients. The butcher did by selling rationed meat to Darlene and others who could pay dollars for it. Tanya's mother sometimes rented rooms to Darlene's friends, young and poor *jineteras* who came from the eastern provinces and lived in quarters too crowded to do business. But Pablo wasn't a fighter. A graduate from Havana Law School, he worked in a local *Notaría*, marrying and divorcing people. He was an unrepentant loser, Ana screamed, *un pobre diablo* with no balls.

Menina loved and pitied him, yet she couldn't
describe her feelings for the woman she used to call
Mamá. She had a vague memory of being afraid of her
because Ana scolded Menina often and complained
that the girl was getting too spoiled. In Havana,
Luisa was around to protect her and to veto Ana's
punishments. Luisa had always been *la mandamás*,
the boss. She was the owner of the house, the one who
distributed food and had the last word. But in San
Diego, Ana would likely be *la mandamás* and Menina
couldn't help feeling apprehensive.

The plane landed and Pablo grabbed his
daughter's hand. He seemed more nervous than when
they had arrived in Miami. Just like Menina, he was
afraid of Ana. He would be in her turf now, and his
mother was dead.

Menina felt a tinge of embarrassment as Pablo
dragged their old wooden suitcase down the plane
aisle. She hid her vinyl purse under one arm, hoping
nobody noticed it. Though they had had a foretaste
of other people's travel luxuries at the Miami airport,
the excitement of being in a foreign country for the
first time had overpowered any other feeling. The
uncomfortable sense of being "less than" had soon
subsided, but it was coming back with a vengeance.
Everybody carried modern rolling suitcases, Menina
realized somberly. Everybody except them.

To make things worse, her pink polyester dress,

highly fashionable in Havana, seemed cheap and shabby compared to the crisp jeans and cotton blouses that other girls around her own age had. And when she looked at shoes... *ay*, then she wished she could just walk barefoot instead of having those awful plastic sandals that nobody else wore!

They started looking for the exit but found so many confusing signs that Pablo, disoriented, stopped and asked for help in faltering English to a security guard. Menina wished she could ask someone for help too.

Should I still call Ana Mamá*? It's going to sound strange. When we talked on the phone I never did because grandma was around and she had become my new mom. But now...*

Her reflections were cut short by an unexpected hug. A floral fragrance enveloped her and a well-known voice shrieked, "Menincita, my baby! You've turned into a woman on me!"

Menina responded to the hug the best she could. The arms around her shoulders felt like a stranger's, but she managed to say, "*Hola*. I'm glad to see you."

"*Ay, Dios*, you are so tall...and so pretty! Did you have a good trip?"

"Yes."

Ana approached Pablo and patted him on the back, awkwardly.

"I've missed you a lot, *mujer*," he said and kissed her. "Four years is a long time."

Ana's eyes were brighter and more severe than Menina remembered. She didn't return her husband's kiss.

"Let's go," was all she said. "*Andando.*"

While they walked to the parking lot, Menina noticed the aura of assertion that surrounded her mother, her confident strides and her stylish beige pant suit. Her hair, a long brown mane in Havana, was now short-cropped and highlighted, and she had gained several pounds.

The cool evening breeze scratched Menina's face as if invisible pieces of glass were floating in the air. When people made eye contact with her, some smiled for no reason, particularly the women.

Why do they act so friendly if nobody knows me?

Ana guided them through a labyrinth of vehicles. A blue Honda let out a beeping sound that made Menina jump. She caressed the car's polished surface and said, "This looks like a rocket, Ana."

Her mother didn't mind being called by her first name. "It's just a jalopy, *un cacharro*, but it takes me to places. Get in."

Menina sank into the back seat among stacks of papers, books, a drawing pad and two cardboard boxes that smelled of pepperoni pizza. She placed the purse on her lap and felt a warm current that passed through the vinyl fabric. She remembered Maestro's dark, deep eyes and his slender body. Camilo had been so jealous of Maestro, of his relationship with her...

"Do you want me to drive?" Pablo asked.

From behind the wheel, Ana shot him a glance with the same exasperated expression that signaled the beginning of their fights in Havana.

"Are you crazy?"

"Well, I—"

"You don't have a driver license. You don't know the city. And you've never driven an automatic car."

"I can drive any car."

She turned the radio on and a flow of English phrases swathed Menina like a fishnet. It was seven-thirty p.m. and the girl set her watch to Pacific Time.

"Buckle up," Ana ordered. Pablo looked baffled. "Your seatbelt," she said sharply. "Like this," and she pointed at hers. "You too, *niña.*"

Menina fumbled with her seatbelt and Pablo said in an irritated tone that he tried to disguise as joking, "You've become too Americanized, Ana. Awfully bossy."

"I am *not* bossy. It's the law."

They drove away from the airport. There were bright, pulsing lights everywhere—in cars, houses, theaters' marquees, doorways of restaurants and shops. Menina had never seen so many signs, so many colors that embroidered the night...A night in Cuba was always dark, even when they didn't have blackouts. In San Diego, it seemed like a night-day, an in-between, radiant state.

Ana sped up and joined the traffic in the freeway.

Stay at the finest of downtown San Diego hotels,
Menina read. *Welcome to the Grand Hyatt! Visit our
splendid Sunset Cliffs. Come to the San Diego world
famous zoo!* Advertisements had taken the place of
slogans. Instead of fiery-eyed Che Guevara, a blonde
with perfect teeth beamed from a giant billboard.

"Is the city so lit-up all the time?" Menina asked.

"Pretty much," Ana said, "but of course, it's
almost Christmas. People always set up more lights
and stuff at this time of the year."

Menina tried to establish a connection between
Christmas and lights, but couldn't. In Havana,
December 25th was a day like any other. A few families
put plastic Christmas trees and garlands in their
homes and she had once seen a real, ornamented pine
tree at Nuestra Señora del Carmen Church, but there
were no public displays.

A synthetic melody came out from Ana's purse.
Keeping one hand on the wheel, she turned off the
radio, retrieved a cellular phone (the kind Menina had
seen only in movies), held it to her ear and began to
talk. Her sentences were as short and cropped as her
hair. Menina wanted to follow the conversation but
the little English she had learned in Cuba didn't have
anything in common with her mother's curt, broken
syllables. The only word she could identify was her
own name.

"Who was it?" Pablo asked after Ana hung up.

"A friend."

72

Someone honked behind them. Ana cursed in Spanish and hit the accelerator. Menina felt a pain in her stomach and her ears buzzed.

"Slow down!" Pablo yelled.

Ana ignored him, her eyes fixed on the road. Pablo didn't talk again until they left the freeway. This time he addressed Menina, "Are you okay, *niña?*"

"Just fine," she hurried to say.

Menina noticed that some billboards were written in Spanish. Most were ads but one depicted a scary-looking figure, a cross between a fat pig and a well-fanged vampire. It read *Cuidado con el chupacabras!*

"What is *el chupacabras?*" she asked.

"Nothing, just a stupid Mexican invention," Ana answered.

"But... it is an animal?"

"Don't be silly. *El chupacabras* doesn't exist. It's like *el coco* in Cuba, a boogeyman."

The car approached a house surrounded with a picket fence. A string of Christmas lights covered the roof line like silver sequins and the garden had more light bulbs than the entire block where Menina used to live. Even a palm tree was lit up and flashed in a warm, welcome-home manner. Menina's heart leaped.

This is our place! Coñó, *how cool! Wait until I send a picture to Tanya! She isn't going to believe it...*

But they passed by the house, heading instead toward a row of three-story buildings painted brown and pressed against each other like Habaneros at

the butcher's queue. *Anita St. Apartments* read a
discolored outdoor sign. Ana parked the Honda
between a minivan and a VW beetle.

"Why don't you park over there?" Pablo pointed
to a corner. "You have more room." Ana turned off the
engine. "*Mujer*, didn't you hear me? What's the matter
with you?"

Menina braced but Ana said in a casual tone,
"This is an apartment complex, Pablo. Everybody has
a designated spot."

Pablo sighed and bit his lower lip. In Havana,
drivers parked their Chevrolets and Russian Ladas
wherever they found a suitable space, which might
very well be on the curb.

Menina breathed in the night air, cold and
transparent like a piece of glass, and held on to
her purse. All the windows were closed and all the
buildings looked identical. There were no clotheslines
in sight, no sign that anyone lived there, except for the
parking lot full of vehicles.

"Come on!" Ana's voice startled her. "Don't stay
here all night, guys."

Pablo picked up the suitcase and they followed
Ana inside a building. It was the first time Menina
set foot in one where salsa music didn't come from
at least two apartments. The silence was as cold and
uninviting as the chilly Pacific breeze. They took the
elevator up to the third floor. Ana stopped in front of a
white door and opened it.

"*Bienvenidos*!" she said, and Menina perceived a change in her mother's tone and gestures, an effort to sound welcoming and kind. "Come in and make yourselves at home."

II: Two gardenias

Menina and Pablo stepped into a frosted world of white walls, white ceiling and white carpet. A green sofa covered by a yellow quilt provided a lone splash of color and was the only piece of furniture in what appeared to be the living room. A table and three plastic chairs had been squeezed inside the pocket-sized kitchen. The combined living and dining areas were smaller than Menina's bedroom in Cuba. A pungent smell of roses filled the place and Menina sniffed the air, delighted.

"You bought flowers!"

"Actually, it's an air freshener," Ana explained. "Hope it isn't too strong."

Menina looked at her father, who shrugged. But he surveyed the room with a content expression and patted the girl's arm, "We'll find out more. It's our first day, okay?"

Ana led them to a small balcony.

"There is a communal swimming pool, a Jacuzzi and a club house," she said, opening the glass door. "You guys are going to love this place in the summer."

Menina nodded. The sight of a kidney-shaped pool lit up by underwater lamps offset the bad impression caused by the icy, shrinking world that had engulfed them. But the memory of the house in the corner, shining like a giant chandelier, still pained her.

"This place isn't as big as your home in Havana,

but it is… very cozy. And the best I could find, given the circumstances."

"It's great," Pablo answered. "We'll be perfectly fine here, my *amor*."

"Well, *we*…," Ana cut herself off. "Let's look at the rest of the apartment."

She showed them a room furnished with a twin-size bed, a lamp table and a futon. A mirrored closet door occupied one of the walls and Menina caught a glimpse of her own reflection next to her mother's. She was almost as tall as Ana.

"This will be your bed until I can buy something better, Meni," Ana fluffed up the futon. "We'll put it in the living room."

"Am I going to sleep on that?"

"Yes. But don't worry. It's quite comfy once you get used to it."

In Havana, Menina had had her own room and a *real* bed. She pouted and adopted an injured air, but Ana didn't notice.

"Don't you want to wash your face, *niña*?"

Menina brought her purse inside the bathroom. The shower was also undersized but new and clean, unlike their mold-stained Cuban bathtub. Menina peed into a toilet bowl filled with a suspicious-looking bluish liquid. After washing her hands and face with warm water (another improvement) and jasmine soap, she took out the picture and stared longingly at her friends' faces.

"This is nice but… not what I expected, you know?"

"Let's move the futon to the living room now," Pablo whispered to Ana. "We need sometime together. Don't you think, my *amor*?"

"No, Pablo."

"Why not?"

"Like you said, four years *is* a long time."

The couple sat on the edge of the bed and began to talk, first in whispers and then much louder, as the argument got more heated. Menina listened to them from the bathroom, not daring to step out.

Her mother's tone was firm and unapologetic, "I did it for *la niña*'s sake. I didn't want her to grow up in Havana and be like your sister."

Pablo's voice was first angry, then cracking and subdued, "Why didn't you tell me? Why did you send for us? If I had only known…"

"We can still be friends."

"No, we can't."

"Start unpacking," Ana said when Menina opened the door with shaky hands. "You guys must be starving. I'll fix something to eat."

A gloomy look had replaced Pablo's cheerful expression. Menina avoided his eyes and examined the barren walls and the lampless lamp table. She felt the old, familiar weight on her chest dragging her down again. There were no books, no papers, no drawing pads...

"Ana," she said, "don't you draw anymore?"

"I do." The apartment was so tiny that Ana, now in the kitchen, didn't need to raise her voice. "I'm preparing a series on birds."

The last time Menina had seen her mother draw, back in Havana, Ana had filled a notebook with orchids, gardenias, roses and marigolds. Every night after supper she sat at the dining room table and worked on her sketches while Luisa hovered around and frowned. Her upper lip curled, the old woman wondered aloud if her daughter-in-law didn't know that light bulbs and candles were rationed.

"And if you were doing something useful, at least..."

Pablo would call Ana from their bedroom, "*Mujer*, it's late. Come to bed!"

Ana didn't like to be interrupted when she was drawing. Menina remembered one particular night when Luisa had intervened, saying, "Why don't you listen to your husband?"

Without looking up, Ana had flashed her middle finger.

"You're so rude!"

She would keep drawing until midnight, singing ballads. Her favorite was *Dos gardenias* that had become popular again because of the Buena Vista Social Club's latest success.

Pero si un atardecer

las gardenias de mi amor se mueren
es porque han adivinado
que tu amor me ha traicionado
porque existe otro querer.
(But if one evening
the gardenias of my love die
it's because they've guessed
that you have betrayed me
because there is someone else.)

A few days after the middle-finger incident, following a blackout, Luisa had used Ana's notebook to wipe down the water that leaked from their old Frigidaire.

"It was so dark that I mistook it for old papers," she said.

Menina suspected she had done it on purpose. So did Ana, and she was mad for weeks. *Ay*, all her orchids and gardenias drowned in the smelly dark fluid that oozed from rotten chicken thighs!

"Let me see your drawings," Menina walked into the kitchen.

"Supper is almost ready," Ana said, spreading butter on a muffin. "Turkey and gravy, something you've never tasted." She got closer to Menina and hugged her. "I'm really happy you came, Meni. Sorry if I sounded... a little impatient. I'm not angry at you, *entiendes*? I'm just nervous and frazzled and tired. The last months have been very, very difficult for me.

But I'm delighted that you guys made it here."

Menina nodded. "I'm happy too, Ana," she lied.

"You'll get used to San Diego. It's one of the most beautiful cities in the country."

"Yes, it looks nice. Not at all like Havana.

"You bet."

"So… where are your drawings?"

"In my studio."

"What is a studio? Is it far from here? May I see it?"

"Don't ask so many questions, *chica*," Ana hugged her again and Menina noticed for the first time the wrinkles that encircled her mother's eyes. "*Oye*, you sound like a reporter. I'll take you there someday."

The microwave oven made two short buzzing noises. Menina turned to see it. Luisa had wanted to buy one but they were too expensive, even for Aunt Darlene's pocket.

"Did you pay a lot of *fulas* for this, Ana?"

"Dollars, Menina. We use dollars, not *fulas*, in the United States. And it came with the apartment."

"With the apartment? The family that lived here before gave it to you? Because in Cuba people have to carry the refrigerator, the stove and everything else when they move to a new place, don't you remember?

"You aren't in Cuba anymore, sweetie. Life is different here. No one 'gave' anything to me. We are just renting this place."

"Renting? From whom?"

"I don't know his name. From the complex's owner."

"The complex? What's the complex?"

"Please, Menina! No more questions for now. I'll try to explain everything new to you, but not at once.

"I just wanted to know…"

"You are giving me a headache!"

Ana forced a smile but Menina realized her mother was on the verge of losing her temper.

"Sorry."

"Go help your dad unpack."

She dragged her feet back to the bedroom. Pablo had emptied the suitcase. A denim skirt, a pair of jeans, a nightgown and two blouses—all the clothes that Menina had brought—were hanging in the closet. "No one brings old stuff to *La Yuma*," Menina had said before leaving Havana, offering her entire wardrobe to Tanya. "Here, take whatever you want."

Pablo coughed before asking in an exaggeratedly joyful tone, "Well, how do you like San Diego and this pretty apartment?"

"I don't like it at all," Menina lowered her head. "This place feels like no one's home."

"It was no one's home, but it'll be ours from now on."

"Ours."

"Yours and mine."

"What about her?"

"Ana has her own place and—a new boyfriend.

She isn't going to live with us, but you can visit them if you wish."

Boyfriend? Visit? Wish?

In the kitchen, Ana began to hum *Dos gardenias.* Menina burst into tears.

"Some first day in America," Pablo muttered.

Pero si un atardecer
las gardenias de mi amor se mueren.
es porque han adivinado
que tu amor me ha traicionado
porque existe otro querer.

83

III: From ration cards to credit cards

The tree towered over the carrousel, its ornamented branches stretched to the sky. *On the fifth day of Christmas* Menina looked up/ m*y true love sent to me* multicolored lights *five golden rings* danced around her *four calling birds/ a* silver star twinkled *three French hens* above her head/ people walked fast without paying attention *two turtle doves and* only children seemed interested in the plastic foliage that kept *a partridge in a pear tree* Menina's eyes glued to its blinking surface.

She had asked her father for a Christmas tree but Ana, *la entrometida*, had said no way, you don't need a tree, *chica*, that's a waste of money, there is no space in the apartment plus the season is almost over. Almost over, on December the 22nd! Menina had thrown a tantrum, only to be told by her mother that she was "too grown up for making such a scene…"

A gentle rain had fallen in the morning but the sun finally came out and now it looked like a fluorescent lamp hanging from a cobalt ceiling. Menina wished she could paint as well as her mother to portray the beauty of the day.

After lunch, Ana had driven her daughter and Pablo to Mission Valley shopping center, near her condo, which neither of them had yet visited. Menina had never seen a mall and took everything in. She felt that she needed and deserved a break.

The first two weeks of her San Diego stay had been filled with nonstop fights. Her parents kept hurling recriminations and insults at each other and sometimes forgot she was there too... just like it used to be in Havana, but minus Grandma Luisa and Tanya.

She could repeat their mutual accusations word by word.

"You lied to me! You never said you had another guy."

"I did it for Menina. There was no future for her in Cuba. She couldn't even count on *you*."

"You are a loose woman."

"And you aren't even half a man!"

But they had signed an armistice. They had gone out twice to a Japanese restaurant called Kaga Sushi (the name always made Menina giggle because Kaga sounded like "shit" in Spanish) and Ana had found a job for Pablo, cleaning floors and shelving tools in a hardware store.

The shop belonged to a Salvadorian, a soft-spoken old man that paid him eight dollars an hour. Eight dollars an hour! At first Menina thought that it was an exorbitant amount—in Havana, one could buy a two-week supply of groceries for a family of four with a hundred dollars—but soon she realized that, as Ana had said, life was different in the United States. Since Pablo worked only three days a week, his income wasn't enough to cover even their eight-hundred dollar monthly rent. Ana came up with the rest of the money.

"This is only a temporary situation," Pablo reassured Menina. "When I get papers, I'll start making more."

Menina didn't know exactly what kind of papers he was referring to, but hoped he got them soon. She didn't like having to ask Ana to buy her everything, from toilet paper to a pair of panties.

On a positive note, the apartment looked more like a home now. Ana had brought a television set, a rocking chair, a cordless phone and a glass-top table. Menina placed her friends' picture on the table, propped against a soda can, and decided that her first purchase would be a frame for it. Tanya's contagious smile never failed to remind her that she was in *La Yuma*, after all. She'd better be grateful.

While Ana and Pablo sipped cappuccinos outside Robinsons-May, Menina went for her first taste of a shopping spree. With twenty-five dollars folded inside her new XOXO handbag (Ana's pre-Christmas gift, because the other one, the Cuban vinyl purse, had been discarded), she felt ready for an adventure in that magical world where one didn't need a ration card to shop.

She hesitated at the Robinsons-May's threshold. The tall, blond and well-dressed clerks intimidated her, but the tantalizing mix of sweet smells and glitter prevailed. She took a few tentative steps, zigzagged around the perfume counters and found herself inside the brightly lit fashion jewelry department. She touched an imitation pearl strand with a finger and gaped at the price tag.

Twenty six dollars! Forget it. Let's see this pair of earrings. Thirty-two... maybe they are real diamonds. Wait, it says they are on sale. That means cheaper. I'm going to ask.

But when a six-foot saleswoman approached her, Menina dashed out of the store. Her heart was pounding.

I shouldn't run like that. She might have thought I was stealing something, or planning to. Oye, it would be so easy to steal here. Things are—available, waiting for you to take them, unlike in the Havana dollar shops where jewelry is under lock and key and there are security guards everywhere. I could just slip that pretty necklace inside my purse. Wait, I'll take two *necklaces, one for me and the other for Tanya. But that clerk already saw me. She will find it suspicious if I return now.*

The girl started walking toward another shop.

"Come back soon," Ana shouted at her. "Be careful and stay around!"

Menina shrugged, but even if she had had her parents' permission, she wouldn't have ventured too far away from them. During the last two weeks all local TV stations had been running stories about *el chupacabras*. Not the boogeyman or the mythical creature that scared misbehaving children, like *el coco* in Cuba, but a serial killer who had already murdered five girls, three of them Hispanic. Their bodies had been found in the Chula Vista outskirts, with wounds in their necks, their hair torn out and the word *chupacabras* written with blood over their disfigured faces. This was the first time that Ana and Pablo allowed Menina to go anywhere by herself and she could feel her father's anxious gaze following her among the crowd.

She sensibly avoided a toy shop. Three days before, at K-Mart, she had convinced Ana to buy her a Barbie doll set with a washable poodle that lost its charm after the second bath. Menina still regretted it.

Sorry I wasted fifteen dollars on that crap when I don't need toys anymore. I am going to be fifteen in four months. I'm a woman!

The clerks at Charlotte Russe were younger, shorter and less intimidating than the Robinsons-May saleswomen. A perky girl about Menina's age smiled at her. "May I help you?"

"I no speak English well," Menina said.

"*¿Hablas español?*"

"Yes. I mean, *sí*. You too?"

"Sure. *Vente* with me."

The salesgirl, whose nametag read Cathy, made herself understood in a peculiar mix of English and Mexican Spanish.

"Everything is on sale," she pointed to a rack full of summer clothes. "You get a *cincuenta* percent discount. *Qué padre*, no? *Mira*, this is *bien chido*," she handed Menina a flowered dress with a V-shaped neckline. "Come see our fitting room."

After trying on three dresses, a leopard print coat with a fake fur collar and a pair of suede boots, Menina's head was spinning. The dresses cost ten dollars each; she could buy two and still have five dollars left. Unfortunately, they were short and Pablo didn't want her to wear miniskirts. The boots looked good but felt hard inside, almost like orthopedic shoes. She did like the coat, though. It was the most luxurious piece of clothing that she had ever worn.

Menina stared at a poster where a dark-haired, impossibly skinny woman sported that same coat.

"This *abrigo* is so cool," Cathy said. "I have one myself and wear it all the time. And it's a bargain, *tú sabes*? Normally we sell it for seventy dollars, but now *es tan solo cuarenta. El cheapo*!"

"I don't have enough money to buy it," Menina confessed. "I'm sorry."

"Why don't you put it in a credit card?"

"What's that?"

Ten minutes later Menina, brimming with excitement, rushed out of Charlotte Russe. *Even if Ana doesn't have the money right now, she can still buy me the coat.* Qué padre, *as Cathy said. That's a nice*

*American practice. Will people use these cards all the
time or only during Christmas?*

Menina had even forgotten about *el chupacabras.*
Her mind wrapped around the American credit card
system, she took the wrong turn and ended up in front
of the AMC 20 Theaters entrance. *Twenty theaters?
Does it mean that they show twenty different movies at
the same time?*

She passed by Ruby's and stopped to admire
the larger-than-life figure that stood in front of the
cafeteria like a smiling giantess. *She's almost as big as
the bearded guy that they put near the Christmas tree.
What's his name? Santicló? Ay, mi madre, I'm going to
be late and Ana will be so pissed off so she won't give
me a cent more or let me use her card!*

Menina was on the verge of tears when she finally
caught sight of her parents.

"Where in the world were…?" Ana began to say,
but Menina didn't let her finish.

"I just tried on the most beautiful fur coat and I
only need fifteen more *fulas,* I mean, dollars, to buy it!
Or we can put it on a credit card."

"It can't be a real fur coat for that price, *boba,*"
Ana replied. "By the way, who's been telling you about
credit cards?"

"Cathy, a new friend. She said I could use your
Visa or MasterCard in the store where she works."

"You'll have to learn the difference between
friendship and business, dear. This isn't Cuba, where

clerks bark at the customers and shoo them off the shops. Here, all they want is to sell you something. They *aren't* friends."

Her mother's amused tone annoyed Menina.

"What do you know? You weren't there when we met! She was real nice and offered me a fantastic discount. Now, will you give me—?"

"No, *señor*! Limit yourself to the amount that you have."

"But we don't need to pay for the coat *now*," Menina insisted. "You have until the end of February to send money to the card company. Or you can send them only the… the I-don't-know-what payment."

"Listen to her!" Ana lifted her hands in mocked horror. "Your daughter already knows about minimum payment!"

Pablo grinned proudly. "She's a smart aleck, isn't she?"

"So, may I buy the coat?"

"No! I'm still paying for your travel expenses and that's almost two-thousand dollars," Ana had become serious. "Get something else, or better save your money until next week. Prices will be even lower."

But Pablo was so impressed by Menina's newly acquired knowledge of *La Yuma* finances that he reached for his wallet and offered her three crumpled five-dollar bills.

Ana frowned, "Hey, don't forget you only have a part-time, seasonal job. Besides, *la niña* needs to learn the value of money."

Menina didn't wait for her father's response. She grabbed the bills and ran back to Charlotte Russe.

Meanwhile, Pablo said, "*Mujer*, don't be so tough. This is Menina's first real Christmas, let her enjoy it. I've never been able to buy her anything she wanted and she is such a good kid—"

"You weren't a practical guy in Cuba, Pablo. And you haven't changed a whole lot."

"Oh, cut it out."

The grand total came to forty-four dollars and eighty cents, the cashier informed Menina with a professional smile. Menina, who had never heard of sale taxes, pretended to count her money, though she knew exactly how much she had. She also knew she couldn't go back to ask for one more cent. Dispirited, she was about to abandon the coat on the counter when Cathy came to her rescue. She gave Menina a coupon for another "special discount" that made up for the difference. Promising to return the following weekend, Menina, her new coat on, left the store prancing.

As she made her way through the maze of shops, Menina remembered Maestro and felt a wave of shame. How could she have forgotten him and his teachings so fast? Well, maybe not forgotten, but kept out of her mind... And she hadn't yet bought the frame for the picture! Maestro wouldn't approve of her buying frenzy—the only thing he had in common with the Cuban government's philosophical views was his utter despise for material goods. But Tanya would have loved her new coat, for sure.

Menina retraced her steps with more success than the first time around.

"*Miren!*" she modeled for her parents. "It's lovely, isn't it?

Ana shook her head and chuckled. "Where are you going to wear that thing, Meni, to a carnival?"

The coat started to feel heavy on Menina's shoulders, but Pablo said encouragingly, "You are so pretty, *niña*—like a Hollywood actress!"

She smiled and struck a pose that made her look (she hoped) like the skinny model... or Aunt Darlene. Pablo clapped. Ana rolled her eyes, but ended up laughing. They left the mall together and Menina felt freer and happier than she had for a long, long time. It was as if San Diego had just winked cheerfully at her.

IV: Better than K-Mart

On January the third, Pablo found a new job at a National City warehouse. Now he made four more dollars than with the Salvadorian guy and worked eight-hour shifts, five days a week. Menina understood that they needed the money, but resented the time she spent in the apartment by herself, only accompanied by the flurry of images and sounds that the television spat. She wrote to Tanya almost every week—long, detailed letters about the Anita St. apartment complex, the swimming pool, the flamed grilled chicken from El Pollo Loco, and, above all, the pretty clothes that she found in the mall and those magical, plastic thingies that people called credit cards. But she said nothing about the loneliness that had infected her American life like a virus against which she wasn't immunized.

In Cuba she was seldom alone, even after her mother left. Pablo worked in the *Notaría* from eight to five but Grandma Luisa stayed home most of the day, except when she went to the grocery store or waited in line at the butcher's. If Menina felt bored she just dropped by Tanya's house or sneaked out to visit Aunt Darlene. And there were always lots of people around—walking up and down the streets and seating in parks, sidewalks and bus stops, anywhere she went.

Here, human faces turned out to be a rare sight. The few neighbors she had met were older, busy-looking people. They would smile or wave at her, but didn't even stop to ask how she was doing. In Havana, a foreigner would have been the neighborhood's center of attention for weeks, but in San Diego nobody seemed to care where she was from or what language she spoke. Classes hadn't started yet and Menina hoped that everything would change after she met boys and girls her own age, but in the meantime, life wasn't too much fun. The long, gray shadow of boredom loomed over the Anita St. complex and Menina withered under it.

After the family Christmas party (a short and awkward celebration that included her mother's boyfriend) Menina had only gone out a couple of times, always in Ana's company. *El chupacabras* was still on the prowl and another victim had just been found in Spring Valley, a sixteen-year-old Mexican girl. Pablo wouldn't even let Menina walk by herself to the Laundromat that was around the corner and she was feeling rusty and out of shape, having already gained five pounds. In Havana she used to walk up to three miles a day to avoid the crowded buses, but distances in San Diego were too long. The sidewalks looked empty, buses and cars sped dangerously close to them and now there was *el chupacabras*, to boot.

To keep her entertained, Ana had brought home a bilingual dictionary and several magazines in English. Menina's favorites were those that had to do with cooking, like *Bon Appétit* and *Food Network Magazine*. She even tried to prepare some of the less complicated recipes.

But she missed the exercise, the fresh air and the contact with her old friends. So she phoned Tanya one evening, while Pablo was at work, forgetting that Ana had complained about the cost of her long-distance calls and ordered her to keep them short. Menina talked until her throat ached, whining about her mother and praising the American shops. She knew she had to tell her parents about the call, but kept putting it off. Though she had lost track of time, she suspected that the conversation had lasted at least one hour, maybe longer. Time is money, Ana liked to say, and the phrase had taken another and more tangible meaning lately...

Pablo's Monday shifts started at noon. That morning, as soon as they woke up, Menina begged him to go for a walk.

"I'm getting crazy trapped all day in this apartment, *te lo juro, Papi.*"

"It will have to be a short walk, Meni. I can't miss the eleven o'clock bus."

It was the fifteenth of January, but it felt almost like spring. Wearing t-shirts and sandals, Pablo and Menina strolled around the neighborhood and wondered why they were the only passersby. Pablo seemed more relaxed and Menina thought that *he* needed to get out of the apartment, too. He had been depressed every day after Christmas. Meeting Ana's new partner (an American guy ten years younger than he) had been a blow to his already brittle ego.

"I guess most of our neighbors are working," he said.

"People here work a lot, don't they?"

"Yep."

"Do you like your new job?"

"*Bueno, hija*, it's not the kind of work I'm used to, but as I said, it is just temporary."

"Will it be very difficult for you to be a lawyer again?"

"I think so, Meni, because my English isn't good."

Though Pablo wouldn't admit to it, working in the warehouse had already taken a toll on him. Except for two young Tijuanenses, no one else there spoke Spanish. The overseer was a burly Texan in his thirties who, unlike the Salvadorian, frequently barked at his subordinates. It didn't help that he needed to repeat his orders several times before Pablo understood what was expected of him. Carrying big boxes and arranging heavy items on the shelves was hard work, and the fact that he hadn't done any physical labor during the last ten years made it harder. Even getting up and down a ladder required too much energy and the nimbleness that he didn't have anymore.

"But, God willing, I'll be able to find some kind of office job soon," he concluded and took Menina's hand to cross Palomar Street. "Then we may move to a bigger place so you have your own room again."

Three blocks down the street they discovered a

small, unassuming shop named "Las tres pulgas" and decided to check it out. Menina couldn't believe her eyes when she saw the tag prices. Everything cost less than ten dollars! She got hold of six candles, five cans of mushrooms, two packages of sandalwood incense sticks, three pairs of earrings, a scarf, and a make-up kit.

"We need them anyway, and where are we going to find them cheaper?" she said, as Pablo filled his shopping basket with bars of Palmolive soap, bottles of laundry detergent and toilet paper.

"You're right, Meni. This shop is even better than K-Mart!"

The only clerk, a Mexican woman, addressed them in Spanish, making Menina feel at home. She showed them how to use a can opener just like one they had at home, but couldn't figure out how to operate.

"Do you have picture frames?" Menina asked.

"*Muchos, muy lindos*. Here they are."

Menina chose a plastic golden frame ornamented with pink petals. Pablo didn't complain; it cost only three dollars.

Inside a small freezer Menina discovered ice cream, pie crusts and mixed vegetables. Thinking of a chicken pot pie recipe she had found in the *Food Network Magazine*, she bought a couple of crusts (just in case) and three packages of frozen vegetables. Pablo got two pints of chocolate ice-cream. They walked back to the apartment loaded carrying four big plastic bags.

"So many things, and at much better prices than in other stores," Pablo said. "Why didn't Ana tell us about that little place?"

"Because she doesn't know *everything*," Menina replied, "though she pretends she does."

When they passed by the big house in the corner, a girl dressed in black stared at them from the garden. Not enviously, which would have been the natural reaction in Havana—anybody leaving a dollar-shop with bursting bags would have met his neighbors' jealous gaze—but mockingly. Offended, Menina looked at her sideways.

They had a late breakfast ("a brunch, that's how it is called here," Menina said), and Pablo got ready for work.

"Bye, Meni. I'll be back around nine. Ana will come by and take you to the grocery store. I left a list of what we need on the kitchen, but make sure you cross the items we got this morning."

"Can't we go by ourselves tomorrow?"

"No, sweetheart," he kissed her. "Albertsons's is too far to walk from here. But I'll buy my own car in a couple of months."

"Okay… I'm going to try and make chicken pot pie."

"You go, girl!"

Menina wished her father would get a job in

another *Notaría*, or maybe suing rich people. She had watched enough TV, mostly soap operas, to understand that lawyers were well-paid in *La Yuma*. And they *needed* more money—she had already realized that.

The spring semester was about to start and Ana had registered her at Palomar High School, only five blocks from the apartment complex. Menina was relieved to find out that she wouldn't have to wear a uniform; she used to hate them back in Cuba. Unfortunately, she had asked her mother for better-looking outfits and this had caused another clash.

"Who do you think I am, a millionaire? I still can't understand why you left *all* your clothes in Havana... a coat I had sent you last April, pants that were practically new! What a waste!"

"But you didn't take any clothes with you when you left Cuba, either!" Menina replied.

"Because I came on a raft and there was no space for suitcases there, *comemierda*!"

In the end Pablo bought her two dresses and a blouse at a Goodwill store, and a pair of shoes at Payless. The blouse, though clearly not new, soon became Menina's favorite. The fabric was soft and silky and it had three shades of pink. Only one thing bothered her—the fact that it had cost just five dollars at a shop so, so different from Charlotte Russe or Robinson's-May...

Sometimes Menina felt as if she had been cheated

and she had the strong suspicion that her father did too. True, Ana had never said she was a *millionaire*, but, based on the packages and the money she used to send to Cuba, from two to three hundred dollars every four months, Menina had assumed that her mother was, at least, affluent. Now it turned out that she worked as a receptionist for an architectural firm (she was an architect in Havana, but hadn't been able to validate her degree yet) and took evening classes twice a week in Southwestern College.

"Everything here is done with a computer," she explained to Menina. "I'm still trying to catch up."

Menina, who had never used a computer, got nervous. She also feared that her English wouldn't be good enough and that she would get behind in school.

"You'll also have a lot of catching up to do," Ana said. "But you will. *La necesidad hace parir hijos machos*, you know?"

Necessity forces you to give birth to male children. Menina repeated that old Spanish saying, trying to grasp its meaning. She wasn't planning to have children, male or female, any time soon.

V: Maestro, can you hear me?

Menina dressed as carefully as if she were going to a Saturday night party. She wore her pink blouse and her best jeans, and applied a bit—just a bit, so her mother wouldn't complain—of mascara to her eyelashes. She picked a lipstick color that matched the blouse and added rouge to her cheeks. The make-up kit had been a great choice.

Then she set the stage—she placed five red candles on the floor, flanked by two glasses containing incense sticks. Her friends' picture was in the center, looking much better in its new golden frame. The aroma of burning incense merged with the smell of the chicken pot pie that she had managed to bake using the store-bought crust and El Pollo Loco leftovers. She sat on the floor, closed her eyes and felt as if she were back in Havana.

The candles burned slowly, leaving pearly drops on the carpet and smoke filled the room like a bluish ghost. The sandalwood scent tickled the girl's nostrils and evoked memories of the Cosmic Brotherhood weekly sessions she had attended for two years. *It was after a session when Camilo kissed me for the first time, but I didn't like his tongue or the kiss. The whole thing seemed so gross.*

Every Wednesday evening the Cosmic Brotherhood met in Tanya's house. (Though Tanya's mother, Aurora, didn't believe in the otherworld and made fun of their attempts to contact the astral plane, she welcomed Maestro and his following to make sure that her daughter stayed safely at home.) In their backyard, under a palm tree and in the company of ants, crickets and occasional cockroaches, they called to spirits and Ascended Masters and lit stubs of candles—if there were some left after the blackouts. Occasionally Darlene, who had asked them to "keep her in the light," brought incense sticks provided by her foreign friends.

The Cosmic Brotherhood was a small, motley crew. Besides Menina and Tanya there was Társila, a woman in her forties who wore granny glasses and walked around muttering old ballads under her breath. She had once channeled John Lennon's spirit, singing the whole Beatles repertoire so loudly that the neighbors protested and Aurora threatened to kick the Cosmic Brotherhood and its ghostly guests out of her house. The male gender was represented by Maestro, Paquito (a young man who often reeked of pot) and David the photographer, the oldest guy in the group.

Sessions usually began with an invocation to Saint German; after that, Maestro greeted all the spirits present. (He would speak English when the latter happened to be Americans or British.) Then he would talk for a long time, his syrupy, baritone voice spilling over the attendees like a stream of honey, until they felt the hairs on their necks raise and a vibration in their throats—the symptoms that preceded a manifestation, Maestro had taught them.

Manifestations could be individual, when someone—generally Maestro or David—channeled a spirit and conveyed his or her message to the others. Joan of Arc, Edgar Cayce and Walt Whitman were regular visitors. But they were also public, like the day the Archangel Saint Michael appeared to everybody (well, to *almost* everybody) and addressed them in a clamorous voice.

Menina had never felt or seen a thing that could be called supernatural. She and Tanya were still untrained souls, Maestro said with a smile, and spiritual babies. But she was also a dedicated student and the hostess's best friend, so Maestro had included her in the group. She was honored to be part of the brotherhood, even after Camilo, *el descreído*, told her that no one there experienced anything out of the ordinary and that Saint Michael's apparition was a case of collective hysteria. But they all knew that Maestro could travel astrally and that David and Társila had had several out-of-body experiences.

"Non-believers like Aurora and your friend have trouble making contact with higher planes," Maestro told Menina. "That's normal. Camilo will be skeptical until the day I show up in his room when he least expects it."

Menina thought of asking why he hadn't done it already, but she knew better. An advanced soul, Maestro wasn't fond of showing off his *saddhis*, or spiritual powers.

The evening of the kiss had started as usual. The
Cosmic Brotherhood members were sitting on the
earth, under the palm tree. Menina felt the tickling
of dried leaves under her shorts and Camilo's warm
breath on her neck. (Maestro allowed him to join them
sometimes out of deference to Menina.) It turned out
to be a special session, with an exceptional number of
manifestations. First came a Native American warrior
who stomped his feet and let out a terrifying war
cry. "He was a Navajo," Maestro explained after the
spirit, who had used David as a medium, vanished. A
Taíno Indian followed, humbly asking for a piece of
casabe—yucca cake—but all they could offer him was
a slice of stale bread.

"We don't even have food for us, how are we
going to feed those lazy spirits?" Aurora protested.
"*No jodan*!"

An African slave showed up, brandishing an
invisible machete. A runaway from a Pinar del Río
tobacco plantation, he worshipped the orisha Oggún
and demanded a sip of rum and the last American
cigarette from a package that Paquito had bought in
the black market. Reluctantly, the guy parted with his
Marlboro. Maestro didn't like it when the spirits of
Santeria practitioners came forth during the sessions.
He claimed they were rude, vulgar, undeveloped
and dense. *Santeros* dwelled in such a lower level
that it was almost impossible to keep a meaningful

conversation with them, yet they were too powerful to be dismissed or ignored.

After the African slave retreated to the spirit world, leaving David exhausted, Menina and Camilo excused themselves and said good-by. Menina wanted to slap him. He had been snickering during most of the session and looked at David and Maestro as if the two were freaks. *Qué irrespetuoso*! Before they turned the corner, Camilo, laughing uncontrollably, informed Menina that the manifestations were *pura mierda de perro*, dog poop in its purest state.

"Don't you see that old David was putting on a show, Meni? All his 'Indians,' Taínos and Americans, spoke exactly the same way and had identical war cries. His African slave sounded just like Pedrito, the Los Van Van lead singer. And how come the spirit asked for a Marlboro? Did they have *Yuma* cigarettes in his times? Aurora was right. *No jodan*!"

Menina walked away, upset. Camilo ran after her.

"I'm sorry, Meni," he whispered. "I didn't intend to offend you. I'll come back if you want me to."

He kissed me and from that day on we were novios. *I never told* Papi *because he had already said that I was too young to have a boyfriend... I lied to him, said I was hanging out with Tanya when I was with Camilo. And then he took me to his house, where we did* cuchi-cuchi *for the first time. It hurt. Ay, did it hurt! It was nothing sweet or beautiful or awesome, as other girls said it should be, only pain and blood.*

A mess. After a while it stopped being so painful, but it was never anything—special. I had more fun during the Cosmic Brotherhood meetings than in bed with him. Maybe there is something wrong with me.

But only three months later Camilo dumped her for a taller girl who was more experienced and probably better at *cuchi-cuchi.* At least that was Menina's opinion, but the real reason could have been that she was already planning to leave Cuba and *he* didn't want to be the one dumped. Or that he considered her a traitor to the revolution... Menina cried for weeks and swore not to look at guys anymore. Maestro tried to reassure her but not even him, or the spirits, could help.

"Don't worry, Meni," Tanya said. "Get yourself a *Yuma* boyfriend and then come back with him. Camilo will die of jealousy."

Menina giggled now, recalling Tanya's words. She hit a candle with her right heel. It tipped over and the flame began to lick the carpet but the girl, her eyes still closed, couldn't see it.

A Yuma boyfriend! Well, why not? There will be plenty of guys at the new high school. Why can't I meet a nice boy and go out with him? I want one... with blue eyes! I've always liked blue eyes.

A shrill sound took Menina by surprise. It cut like a razor blade through her ears and she began to shake. Though she had often asked and prayed for a manifestation, its imminence scared her.

Forgetting the prospective boyfriend, the girl remained motionless, struggling to breathe, suffocated by the veil of smoke that had spread over the room.

"You came here astrally, as you promised," she whispered. "I knew you would. Dear Saint German, protect Maestro. Ascended Masters, guide him during his astral trip. And guide me too!"

The noise got louder. It didn't seem to come from any particular point in the space, but filled the entire apartment and Menina's throbbing skull.

"Are you here, Maestro? Can you hear me? I was waiting...waiting for you."

Someone was at the door. The lock clanked but Menina didn't hear it.

"Sorry it took me so long to do a ceremony. I don't know if Tanya told you, but I've been..."

"What the hell is going on?" Ana came in and hurried to throw the yellow quilt over the flames. "What are you doing, Menina? Are you okay?"

Slowly, as if awakening from a deep sleep, Menina looked around and found her mother standing in the middle of the room.

"Uh...yes."

Ana opened the balcony screen. The noise became less audible, until it mercifully stopped.

"Can you please tell me what this means?" Ana took Menina by the shoulders. She wasn't angry, but frightened, and her face had turned the color of the living room walls. "Who brought these candles here?

Did anyone give them to you?"

"*Papi... Papi* and I bought them."

"Why did you put them on the carpet? Didn't you see the flames or hear the smoke alarm, for God's sake?"

"The smoke alarm," Menina repeated. It wasn't a question. She was just trying to make sense of her mother's words and Maestro's aborted arrival. "Did that thing—make the noise?"

"Of course, *hija*! That's what it's for, smoke activates it. But what were you doing? Praying?"

"I was just calling—calling Maestro," Menina ran to the bathroom and closed the door behind her.

"Wait! Who's Maestro?"

Doubled over the sink, the girl choked back her tears.

Maestro can't materialize, can't travel astrally, can't do shit. Spirits don't exist. Everything he said was a lie and Camilo, the bastard, was right.

Ana sighed audibly, picked up the burned quilt and put it back on the sofa. She looked at the picture and recognized Tanya, but wondered who the tall, skinny, long-haired guy was. She blew out the candles, threw them and the incense sticks into the garbage can and, with another sigh, took the vacuum cleaner out of the closet. Then she saw the chicken pot pie on the kitchen counter and her expression softened.

"Menina! Come here and let's talk, girl!"

An hour passed. Menina came out of the bathroom, plopped down on the sofa and refused to answer her mother's questions.

"Okay, it was an accident," Ana said. "I understand, Meni, I really do. But I'd like to find out—we have been separated for so long that I hardly know you anymore. Do you believe in Santeria or something of that sort? Is that guy in the picture a *babalawo* or an *espiritista*?"

Menina didn't feel like discussing the Cosmic Brotherhood practices with Ana, much less talking about Maestro. She almost wished the shrill noise returned, so she didn't have to hear Ana's voice.

"Would you like to go to a church? We can look for one around here..."

She just wanted her mother to leave the apartment and take with her the smell of incense and burned wool. She felt angry, ashamed and, worst of all, betrayed.

Why didn't anybody tell me about the smoke alarm? These damned American devices!

At first she didn't know how to turn on the microwave or the video player. Even the telephone, with so many little buttons and a lit-up screen, baffled her. Ana taught her to use it and wrote down what she called "an emergency number," warning Menina to dial it only if she was in *real* trouble.

"*Bueno*, let's go and get groceries," Ana said. "You may find your tongue on the way to the store...

Oh, have you guys gotten any new bills?"

Menina shrugged. Ana went out and returned with a bunch of letters, papers and ads.

"Tell your father to pick the mail up every two days or the mailbox will get too full," she said, but Menina didn't seem to hear her.

While Ana opened some envelopes and discarded others, the girl kept her eyes fixed on the floor. She didn't see when her mother pursed her lips and looked closely at a piece of paper.

"Don't ever do that again, *niña*!" Ana screamed, the previous softness gone. "No more calls, *coño*! No more calls!"

Menina jumped up from her seat.

"What? Are you talking about... about Maestro?"

"*Qué* Maestro *ni un carajo*? Look at this! A three-hundred-dollar phone bill! Who made that call? I don't think your father is *that* senseless, so it must have been you. Calling Cuba is expensive! And it went on for one hundred and twenty minutes, damn it!"

She already knows for how long I talked, down to the minute! Ay, Dios, one has to be careful here in La Yuma, *where even telephones tell on you. This is worse than living next to the Committee for the Defense of the Revolution!*

"*Niña*, was it you? It could be a mistake but I doubt..."

"Yes, I called Tanya," Menina's tears fell down, despite her efforts to hold them back. "*Papi* was

111

working, you were not here and I was feeling sad. I didn't know it would be so expensive." She rubbed her mascara-smeared cheeks. "I'm sorry."

"*Oye*, Menina," Ana sat next to her and made an effort to speak calmly again. "I know that you miss Tanya and your friends in Havana, and I wouldn't have minded the call if you had limited your conversation to ten or fifteen minutes. But two hours, *chica*! You need to learn how to control yourself."

Menina lowered her head. "Are you going to tell *Papi*?"

"*Papi*? Who cares about your *Papi*, silly? What he makes, listen to this, what he makes is barely enough to cover your rent. All the other expenses— gas, electricity, food, phone...you name it—are paid by *me*!"

Menina's tears stopped.

"If you are going to rub it on our noses, then stick your dirty money up your ass, *bruja, mala*! I'm so sorry we ever came!"

She regretted having said such words as soon as they came out of her mouth, but wouldn't take them back. Ana looked at her in disbelief, shook her head ominously and went into the bedroom. Menina heard her open the closet and search inside the drawers.

What is she doing? Bah, I don't care. I know what we are going to do. We'll go back to Cuba! I'll sell my new clothes there and get enough fulas *to support* Papi *and me for a year.*

112

Ana came out carrying a plastic bag.

"Now we'll see if I am a witch and if I am bad," she seethed. "*Pues*, you aren't keeping any Christmas presents, how's that? You need to be taught a lesson because you're getting too *hocicona*. I'll take all this back to the stores to help pay for the phone bill."

"You can't do that!" Menina tried to snatch the bag from Ana's hand. "*Papi* paid for that coat! And he bought my new sandals, not you!"

"*Papi* hasn't paid for a thing, *estúpida*! We aren't in Cuba anymore! Here, you do things my way or you hit the highway."

The last sentence sounded like an oral puzzle, but Menina didn't have time to put it together. Pablo came in, looking dejected and more tired than usual. Before he could say anything, he found himself in the middle of the female crossfire.

"The silly girl, spending three hundred dollars in a phone call and insulting me after I am!"

"The *bruja* wants to take my clothes back to the store! She hates me!"

"If you dare call me a *bruja* again, I'll slap you!"

"Leave us alone!"

"Shut up!"

But Pablo didn't take Menina's side, as she had fully expected. Instead of defending her and her belongings from Ana's wrath, he said, "You have to respect your mother, *mija*!"

"I haven't disrespected her."

"Yes, you just did. Go to the bedroom."

"But *Papi*, let me explain to you"

"Go to the room, I said! You are grounded!"

That was too much for Menina to bear. She ran away, hit the stairs and didn't stop until she was outside the building. She heard voices that called for her: "Menina! *Niña!* Come back!" but she ignored them. She walked fast, hoping to reach the corner before her parents saw her.

I won't let them catch me. I'm leaving them forever, and leaving that ugly, cold, horrible apartment! Wish I had never set foot in it. Oh, here they come!

Her only shelter was the house in the corner. She opened the gate and sneaked in the garden.

I've had enough of them. I'll get a job and move on my own, or return to Havana. If nothing else, I'll live with Tanya and Aurora, or at Aunt Darlene's place.

VI: *Take on me*

Menina hid behind the palm tree. It still had a
string of Christmas lights around and she realized
that they weren't as pretty as they had seemed the
first night. The light bulbs were too big and dull, and
looked like accomplices in a secret conspiracy. She felt
that everybody and everything had failed or betrayed
her—Maestro, her father, Ana…*La Yuma* itself.

Ana and Pablo walked fast by the house, talking
loud, their eyes darting around, their faces pale.

Que se jodan. *Let them look for me, get really,
really nervous. They think I'm going to be waiting for
them at the Anita St. bus stop. Ah, if that bus could
take me right back to Havana, then I would be there…*

Someone opened a window and a girl's voice said,
"It's too stuffy here."

The idea of being caught hiding under the tree
made Menina shudder.

What if they take me for a thief and call 911?

She waited a couple of minutes and sneaked
back to the street. It was getting dark now but she
didn't care. She ran in the opposite direction to the
apartments until her legs began to hurt and she had to
slow down.

Where am I going?

She walked four more blocks, the longest blocks
that she had ever walked, and got into unfamiliar
territory—a strip of nothingness limited by what

appeared to be a small village made up of doll-like houses. There was a taco shop around two hundred feet from the first house. The menu was printed on the walls in black letters, under the red, white and green Mexican flag: *Carnitas, machaca con huevos, tacos, carne asada burritos.*

A woman with an apron stood outside the store, talking to a man who held two plastic boxes in one hand a beer in the other. An old orange Mustang was parked nearby, with the driver's door open and a melody spilled from it, the chords of a sticky A-ha song that Menina used to listen to in Cuba. *But that's me stumbling away* she avoided a hill of old rubber tires *slowly learning that life is OK.* Empty cans, broken bottles and rocks were scattered around.

This looks like an Old Havana neighborhood, as dirty and almost as run down.

The playful city wink she had seen at the mall had been replaced by a menacing grin.

When the desolated strip ended, Menina found herself in front of a banner that read "Welcome to the Sun Valley Estates." She crossed the gate, passed by a fenced pool and approached a small mobile home that had a brown plaster Chihuahua on the porch. From the living room window Menina saw a young woman making pancakes while a man played with a toddler on the floor. The aroma of fried dough filtered out. The woman turned around and said something. The man laughed and even the child made gurgling, happy sounds. The scene sent a throb of pain through Menina's heart.

Were Papi *and Ana ever like that? Did I use to laugh with them?*

Then she noticed someone's presence. It came to her as a quivering of the soul, an intimation of danger carried by the evening air. She couldn't hear anything, she couldn't see anybody, but a knot in her throat and the raising of her neck's hair (the main symptoms of a manifestation, according to Maestro) sufficed. She didn't even try to find out what had scared her, but turned her back to the window and started to run while unconnected thoughts crossed her mind.

Ana was a bitch for yelling at me. She only cares about money. And Papi *didn't raise a finger to defend his poor daughter,* el cobarde! *Why didn't I ask that couple for help? Now I'm in trouble and it is getting dark. What's the number?* I'll be gone *and they will wonder where I went. That A-ha song, Take on me, Tanya used to play it all the time.* I'll be gone in a day or two. *The number—911!*

She was already feeling short of breath but the footsteps behind her (faster, stronger now) propelled her forward. She gained the entrance of the Sun Valley Estates and stopped. The steps stopped too. She wasn't chased, Menina thought, comforted; she was only being *followed.*

I'm going back to the apartment. When Papi *and Ana get tired of looking for* "la niña," *they will go*

117

*home and find me there. That's going to be a good
joke. And I won't talk to any of them for a week!*
Is it life or just a play. *A play. After all, I didn't do
anything too bad. I'll start babysitting and pay for my
phone calls myself.*

She hurried up, trying not to hear the steps,
trying not to think about them. Her chest hurt *you're
shying away* but she ran, she ran *I'll be coming for
you anyway.*

The taco place was silent and the bright colors of
the Mexican flags had turned gray. The waitress wasn't
outside anymore and the client had left.

"*Ayúdeme, por favor!*" Menina tried to yell in
Spanish, but her voice didn't obey her.

A second wind filled her with energy as she
ventured back in the strip of nothingness. She felt
strangely calm, as if she were looking at the scene
(a girl in a pink blouse, running wildly in the dark)
from a vantage point somewhere in the sky. But she
could only see herself. Was someone really chasing
her? Hadn't she left him (it) behind, at the Sun Valley
Estates? *Ay*, if she just dared to turn her head back!
But what if *el chupacabras* was right there with his
vampire fangs and pig head?

Don't be silly. El chupacabras *doesn't exist. It's
like* el coco *in Cuba.*

Menina stumbled over a beer can. She didn't fall,
though. A hand grabbed her before she hit the ground.
She turned around and felt as if the clouds had parted

again to allow her a gloomier, darker glimpse of California's face.

The face that she saw now had steely blue eyes.

* * *

Menina didn't remember how she had gotten there. "There" was a humid little place—not a house, not even a mobile home, maybe just a storage unit. She couldn't see the guy because the place was too dim to distinguish her own shaking, sweat-covered hands, but she could smell him. It was difficult *not* to smell him when he was so close to her, skin against skin, when he was still halfway inside her. And then he said,

"What you doing out so late?"

She had heard him moan and make strange, revolting sounds before, but that was the first time she heard his voice. It was broken and raspy, like the blade of a rusty knife.

"Say, girl, what you doing out?"

"Why you here?" he repeated and slapped her.

"I wanted walking."

He chuckled. "Where you from?"

"Cuba."

"Cuba...that's where that dude Castro is, isn't it? Have you met him?"

Menina closed her legs; her thighs felt sticky and sore. The guy scooted slightly away from her.

"No."

"C'mon! Didn't you see him at least once? I

119

mean, there ain't so many people there. You must have seen him walkin' down the street someday."

Menina's mouth and mind were numb and clogged. All the words had deserted her, both in English and in Spanish. She was hurting and tired. She only wanted to go to sleep and wake up in Havana, in her grandmother's house.

Slowly learning that life is OK.

"Talk to me, little slut!"

She didn't know what "slut" meant, nor did she care.

Life is not OK.

"Hey, you sleeping! Did you see Castro or what?"

"Never met him," she mumbled at last.

Her face was wet. Menina thought she had been crying, but she couldn't remember it. There was a blank slate in her memory that started the moment she had seen the man's blue eyes. She looked for something to wipe her damped cheeks and felt a soft contact under her right arm. It was her blouse. She recognized the fabric, but didn't dare to move and reach for it.

"You didn't?" he let out an exasperated sigh. "That's weird, girl. So, what do you speak in Cuba, Mexican?"

She didn't hear him, wishing she could go back to the moment right before her mother had opened the apartment's door. Or half an hour earlier, when she had lit the candles. But now she wouldn't waste her time calling Maestro. No; she would try to contact Tanya instead.

"You ignoring me?"

He patted her face and the touch of his hand made Menina quiver. It smelled like dirt, blood and urine, among other stenches that she could not identify.

"Eh?"

"What you speak there?"

"*En Cuba hablamos*… Spanish."

What if she tried to reach Tanya *now*? Menina visualized the living room. She saw the green sofa covered with the burned yellow quilt and the vacuum cleaner against the door. She zeroed in on the golden-framed picture that her mother had put back on the table.

Tanya!

"That's Mexican, isn't it?"

She saw Tanya peeking out of the frame, pushing the plastic cover as if it were a curtain and stepping into the room just like the guy in the A-ha video.

"Talk to me!"

She struggled to think of something to say while her friend checked out the television set and the glass-top table. Then she moved to the kitchen counter and discovered the chicken pot pie.

Please, hurry up! Call the police.

Tanya took a bite of the pie.

"Is it Mexican?"

"Yes, yes."

Tanya! Call 911. Just these three numbers: nine-one-one.

"You been to Tijuana?"

Tanya stiffened. Then she turned around and picked up the phone.

"No."

"You don't know *el chupacabras*, then."

To her own surprise, Menina didn't feel afraid. She was looking at the scene from the vantage point once more. But her horizons had expanded; she could see herself and the man inside the storage unit and— all at the same time—she saw Tanya with the phone pressed against her ear.

"No, no *chupacabras* in Cuba."

"Now you're going to meet him."

It was then when she knew that Tanya had heard her, that Camilo was wrong, that the meetings with the spirits under the palm tree hadn't been illusory and that astral travel *did* work. Because how else to explain the bright light, the wailing that sounded like the siren of a police car (or maybe like her own screams) and that wonderful feeling of lightness, of being slowly and safely carried away?

La Llorona's Son

Brenda stands at the threshold and her eyes dart over the tall, blond and somewhat unkempt guy who has just rung the bell. He has old, faded clothes and an undeniable air of loneliness.

"Taylor?" she whispers.

"Yes, Ma."

The young man seems calm—cool, as he would have said in happier times—and doesn't look like someone who disappeared more than a decade ago, leaving an empty space at home.

After the family settled in Albuquerque Taylor grew fond of lying on the grass outside the fence, taking in the immensity of the summer sky. Prairie dogs stood around, as motionless as furry yogis. The boy once caught a sick one and tried to tear his tail off, but it wriggled free. An irrigation ditch flowed nearby and Taylor liked to wash his feet there, though the water never felt warm enough to be enjoyable. The southwest landscape was a discovery for a kid whose only encounters with nature had consisted of Sunday walks around Central Park accompanied by his parents, Brenda and Ed. They had moved to New Mexico in May, when the desert showed its most appealing face. Blooming yucca plants and flowery cacti covered the ground and the sweet tang of the Spanish lavender wrapped the mesas in a fragrant veil.

The irrigation ditch ran behind the house. Neighbors called it *la acequia* and said that La Llorona, the Wailing Woman's ghost, haunted the stream looking for her lost children. Brenda didn't believe (yet) in La Llorona but she had a bad feeling about the ditch since the very first day. She forbade her son to play there and Ed built a tree house to keep him entertained within the limits of their backyard, but Taylor didn't bother to climb into the tree house, not even once.

Fall came. The smell of burned piñón wood rising from the neighborhood chimneys replaced the aroma of Spanish lavender. The cacti lost their flowers. The air got chilly and the prairie dogs hid in their underground villages but Taylor kept sneaking out. He would jump the fence and walk straight to the ditch. Brenda lost count of the times she caught him sitting on the grass, staring at the stream.

"What are you doing here all by yourself?"

"Watching the prairie dogs."

"But they aren't around anymore!"

She couldn't understand what attracted him to the *acequia*. It wasn't until the day Taylor vanished that Brenda recalled La Llorona. The Wailing Woman was an old wives' tale that only uneducated New Mexicans believed in, she used to think. (Because Brenda kept a few East Coast prejudices hidden under her politically correct, fair trade-certified cotton blouses.) Gabriela, her next-door neighbor, pure Nuevo Mexicana, had told Brenda about La Llorona's children, who had drowned in the ditch. "*Su madre*, La Llorona, lost her mind afterwards and began to circle the *acequia*. Now she repeats her cry, *Ay, mis hijos*! to call the poor kids every night." Kids that La Llorona herself might have killed after being dumped by their father, Gabriela added. But it was better not to mention that part of the story. The Wailing Woman's spirit didn't like it when people gossiped about her.

Gabriela knew a song about La Llorona. She taught it to Brenda, who learned to sing it chewing up the terse Spanish syllables,

Dicen que no tengo duelo,
porque no me ven llorar.
Hay muertos que no hacen ruido,
Llorona,
Y es más grande su pesar
(They say that I am not mourning,
because they don't see me cry.
There are dead ones who are silent,
Llorona,
and their pain is even worse.)

The young man is now hesitant and Brenda fears he may go away—again. She forces a smile and lets him in, without saying a word, while her mind races back to that fateful Friday evening at the Balloon Fiesta grounds. She remembers the clouds, the darkness, the balloons that resembled oversize parachutes. Danger was in the air, engulfing everything. She had been able to *smell* it.

It was Ed who insisted on attending the Fiesta. In his self-possessed, affected manner that made Brenda want to scratch him, he had explained why they shouldn't miss the Balloon Glow or the closing firework display. Only once a year... Splendid... We've never seen anything like that... The dramatic effects... Brenda had started to argue but Taylor sided with his father and she gave up. Later on, much later, she recalled her premonition and accused Ed of causing the tragedy, which de denied, of course.

Taylor had just turned twelve years old; he looked younger, almost childlike, with big blue eyes and blond curls. He was quiet, shier than other preteens and hadn't yet shown any interest in girls. Ed wanted to bring up the topic of masturbation in a friendly father-son chat, but Brenda opposed firmly. She longed to shield Taylor from the world, to hide him inside a glass box, Ed complained. But it wasn't as if she had to watch him all the time. Taylor had never gotten in real trouble. He wasn't the kind of kid who would experiment with drugs or get drunk. Or run away from home.

Once at the Balloon Fiesta grounds they had walked around, mildly bored, waiting for the show to begin.

"There are five balloons shaped like dogs," Taylor said. "A Chihuahua, a poodle, a dachshund... but just one like a cat. Why?" he turned to his father in a confiding, little-boy gesture that Brenda loved.

Ed shrugged. "Aren't you getting too old for these idiotic questions?"

Brenda and Ed sat on the folding chairs they had brought from home. Taylor got fidgety.

"I'm going to the candy store."

"Wait," said Brenda. "I'll go with you."

"For God's sake, let him live!" Ed gave Taylor a dollar and winked, "Don't spend all of it in the same place."

Ten minutes later Brenda ran after Taylor while Ed shook his head in mocking disbelief. She couldn't explain why, but felt that her son was in danger. It was a feeling that assaulted her often, heralded by the fast-beating of her heart and a cold sweat, a feeling that prompted her to look for Taylor, to call him, to hug him. It also made Ed grumble, "Geez, you're smothering the kid to death!"

Brenda couldn't find Taylor and went from shop to shop, asking about him and getting crazier by the minute. "You looked like La Llorona," Ed told her that night, the last night they were able to joke together or to talk about Taylor without thinking of La Llorona or empathizing with her one-hundred-year-old pain.

"Here you are!"

Several kids had gathered around a guy who sold toys—plastic, glow-in-the dark balloons, flowers and Kokopellis. The guy wore sunglasses, though it was well past the sunset. As Brenda approached the group the sky exploded in a burst of orange, green and blue sparks. She took her son by the arm and a girl looked at them and giggled.

"Aw, Ma."

"Let's go."

Brenda's anxiety assuaged the minute they moved away from the salesman. The fireworks dissolved like stardust specks in the horizon.

"Why didn't you let me stay there longer, Ma?"

"Because it is too dark."

She had always been vigilant, noticing even the smallest details about her son. Strange that it was Ed who commented about the red plastic balloon that glowed like a firefly nestled in Taylor's hand.

"Did you buy it?"

"Yep."

"How much was it?"

"Uh—one dollar."

"Last year they cost three dollars a piece," Ed said. "It seems like handmade toys don't follow the current trend toward inflation."

"Does inflation have anything to do with the stock market?"

"Now, that's an intelligent question, man."

Ed launched into a lecture about the economy and

it was Brenda's turn to shake her head. A luminous cascade feigned a meteoric rain in the Albuquerque sky.

"How are you?" the young man asks, his voice slight squeaky.

Brenda's pupils dilate.

"Well... and yourself?"

The following morning Taylor refused to accompany Brenda to the Y though he loved its heated, covered swimming pool. He would wake up early on Saturdays and was ready to go even before Brenda finished making breakfast, but when she came into his room that day he hadn't left the bed, at ten to eleven.

"Are you sick?"

"No, tired."

"Do you need anything? What about chicken soup...warm milk?"

"No, no! I am not hungry. I just need to rest."

"But, Taylor..."

"Don't bug me."

This was one of the few impertinent phrases Taylor was known to use. He covered his face, the palms of his hands toward her.

"Okay."

Brenda kissed him on the forehead. He uncovered his eyes but didn't meet hers.

Ed had left early to change the oil in his truck and Brenda saw no logical reason for her to stay home. Taylor was used to being alone. He came back from school at three and Brenda and Ed returned at five-thirty, sometimes at six. Still, while driving down Menaul Street, she felt the same apprehension that had made her hear beat faster the night before, that old, familiar mixture of foresight and concern. *Shouldn't have left the kid alone.* But Saturdays were the only days when she could sweat off her frustrations over the weight-lifting machines, drop her stress on the treadmill, and soothe the cramps of life in the Jacuzzi. Brenda worked as a secretary at the University of New Mexico, in a department where wannabe artists and divas-in-training sprouted every semester like marigolds in her backyard.

When she came home at noon Ed was mowing the lawn.

"Where is Taylor?" she asked.

"Didn't he go with you?"

Brenda tensed up, "No."

The backyard door was opened.

"I bet he went for a walk," Ed said.

"It's too cold."

"Well, then he'll be back soon."

Hours passed. Night fell and Taylor didn't come. The morning brought long searches around the trail, the mesas and inside the irrigation ditch. Brenda and Ed repeated the description they would offer to cops, journalists, neighbors and volunteers—a blond, curly-haired, blue-eyed boy, slender, with an oval birthmark on his chest.

The pressure during the first weeks was agonizing, their days only lit up by a weak ray of faith. And yet those were the days when Brenda and Ed still thought they would be announcing anytime, *You would never imagine where we (they, I, he, she) found him!* The days of calls to the grandmothers, aunts, uncles, and distant cousins in New York and California, some of whom didn't even know Taylor's middle name or how to react to the news. The days when Taylor's picture appeared on the *Have you seen me?* ads and posters, the days of short, disheartening meetings with other parents whose children had vanished months or years before.

Did I do something wrong? Did I drive him away? What kind of mother am I? He must have hated me to leave like that. God, were we so crazy, so... dysfunctional?

These thoughts tormented Brenda, though she hid them from Ed. But he confessed one morning, in bed, after a sleepless night, that they stalked him too. He felt like a failure, he told Brenda, he feared that Taylor had run away because of his poor parental skills. Brenda thanked him silently. Everything became easier for a while. Despite their constant, inevitable pain, their marriage stood stronger than ever, an alliance against the malevolent forces that had robbed them of their child.

They hired a detective and called Missing Children organizations and newspapers and support groups and a Navajo shaman and a Mexican seer and a Cuban *babalawo* and anyone who promised a fleck of optimism. They cried together that Christmas, the first Christmas in twelve years they didn't need to buy toys, and swore to be there for each other, always, no matter what.

But how could she be there for Ed, Brenda asked herself, when he had caused all their suffering? He had insisted on going to the Balloon Fiesta and *that* had put Taylor in contact with the evil salesman, the guy who wore sunglasses in the dark. She knew he had taken her son, though neither the police nor anyone else seemed to understand the connection between Taylor's absence and the glow-in-the-dark toy he had brought home.

"He told us it had cost him one dollar," Brenda repeated. "But I discovered later that they were sold for five. Maybe that guy just gave it to him for free!"

Everybody believed she was paying too much attention to an insignificant detail. Even Ed said that, and it made her so mad that she locked him out of their bedroom for a week, yelling at him, crying like La Llorona. And when spring came the following year she accused her husband of doing everything wrong, not just the night before Taylor's disappearance but all the nights and days of their wrecked married life.

A few months later Brenda heard for the first

time La Llorona's howl *ay, ay, ay mis hijos*. She saw
the woman's shadow around the trail; the trail Taylor
had used to escape, the trail that ended in the *acequia*
where La Llorona's kids had vanished a century
before.

Gabriela taught her the last verse of the song.
Ayer lloraba por verte,
Ay, llorona,
Y hoy lloro porque te vi.
(Yesterday I cried because I wanted to see you,
Ay, Llorona.
And today I cry because I saw you.)

Ed left Albuquerque with the first heat wave of
the summer. He moved to Oakland, remarried there
and only contacted Brenda for a Parents of Missing
Children meeting, or at the request of that private eye
who Brenda loved and hated because he maintained
the boy had left willingly, but didn't deny that
someone (maybe that guy with the sunglasses, yes)
had enticed him to do so.

Brenda wouldn't hear about moving to a smaller
place, though their three-bedroom house had become
the proverbial white elephant now that she was alone.
What if he comes back here, looking for us? She felt
a weird sense of comfort doing the same things she
used to do when Taylor was around. Her job and the
fastidious art students became her only link to life
and sanity. She even helped a young Taos painter put
together a series about La Llorona.

But months and years passed and the Taylor routines, as she called them, dissolved in the new habits of a divorced childless woman. She started to understand La Llorona's rage against the man who had abandoned her and, well, against her own kids too. But she never doubted that Taylor would come back. That was why when the doorbell rang that evening, thirteen years later, her heart leaped. She knew.

Now she tries to smile again at this tall, blond guy who has shown up unannounced. Because she has instantly recognized in his tired, shadow-encircled eyes, the blue ones of her son.

"So, Ma—I guess you weren't expecting this."

This? He sounds and acts so different from the quiet, bashful kid Brenda remembers... she fears for a moment that the young man may be an impostor. She has already had to deal with a certain Rose, a disheveled woman who tried to convince her that a freckled boy she had found by the trail was Taylor, and insisted on getting some kind of compensation. Brenda ended up turning her in to the police. The boy happened to be Rose's own son and there was also a murky story about her drug habits.

"What are you doing?" Taylor backs off when Brenda begins to unbutton his shirt, but she doesn't let go of him until she finds the oval birthmark that Ed had too.

"Come on, Ma, it's me. Really," he pauses. "Hey,

I'm happy that you are still living here. I wouldn't have known where else to look for you."

"I thought so," Brenda says. It dawns on her that she sounds different too. Her voice breaks like an old woman's. "Come in."

She feels a guilty pleasure when Taylor plops down on the couch and doesn't ask about his father, but she finally tells him that they are now divorced. "Because of you" she wants to add, though of course she does not. They exchange polite, hollow words for a few minutes, but when Brenda is ready to ask the inevitable questions Taylor covers his face with his hands, palms outwards.

"Uh, no. Not now, Ma. Please."

She doesn't insist because what else can you do but be quiet and understanding when your only son, your lost child comes back after thirteen years, simply shows up and says Hi, Ma? What can you do, Llorona, but welcome him and pretend you are fine?

She calls Ed, who takes a plane to Albuquerque as soon as he gets off the phone.

"I can't believe it, Taylor!" these are Ed's first words, loud and angry. "Where have you been? Why did you do that to us?"

Funny that he is the one who snaps—always self-controlled, poised Ed.

"Yeah, I left, but why make a fuss now?"

Ed stares at him, shrugs.

135

Taylor wakes up around noon the day after, with a hearty appetite. He devours a couple of fried eggs, four slices of bacon and two muffins. Smiling and refreshed, he praises Brenda's cooking.

They sit in the living room and talk. The scene makes Brenda believe for a moment that time has gone back and they are still the proud parents of a sweet little boy, but the sight of Taylor's six-foot frame kills that thought. He mentions that he lives in San Diego and works in construction and as a handyman. He isn't sure if he will ever go to college, but if he does, he wants to get a BA in art.

"In *art*?" Ed asks.

"I like to do stuff with non traditional materials."

"What's that?"

"Well, uh, human hair, cardboard, empty cans, ribbons…I've made some pieces inspired by the *chupacabras*," Taylor blushes like the shy boy he used to be but changes the subject before Brenda has a chance to comment. "So, Dad, we are kinda close in California."

"Around ten hours by car, I believe."

"Or less, I'm a speed demon."

Brenda feels left out. Jesus, *she* knows a lot about art, both modern and traditional! She wants to say that she could move to San Diego and help her son out in his artistic pursuits, but can't open her mouth. Her tongue has turned as brittle as the tree house that still lays in her marigold-covered backward.

Later Taylor takes a walk by the irrigation ditch and asks about the prairie dogs. "I always dreamed of catching one," he says.

"What for?"

"I don't know."

The three stroll quietly around the burrows and La Llorona's shadow follows them.

It soon becomes clear that all Taylor wanted or needed was a brief, superficial exchange—a sad caricature of the encounter Brenda has dreamed of. He has just dropped by on his way to Miami, where he plans to meet someone whose identity he doesn't reveal.

After his initial outburst Ed seems happy to know that his son is alive and apparently healthy, living a normal life. He doesn't ask any questions, at least not in front of Brenda. He returns to Oakland after giving Taylor a perfunctory hug and his business card. "Now you know where I am. Feel free to visit."

But Brenda can't take it so lightly.

On the third day Taylor just says, "It was nice to see you, Ma, but I have itchy feet."

Brenda sobs alone in her car after dropping him off at the Albuquerque airport. All the questions she has silenced for seventy-two hours now threaten to choke her.

Did you leave with that man? What have you been doing all these years? Why didn't you ever call me?

137

Ayer lloraba por verte,
Ay, Llorona,
Y hoy lloro porque te vi.

Goodbye, Santero

To Victor Goler

*I don't like to be called a santero. See, everybody called
my great grandpa an imaginero; that is the proper term. This
santero word came with the folks who started the Spanish
Market in Santa Fe, gringos who couldn't tell a santo from
a song but they knew people that would buy the santos. And
they said: a santo maker must be a santero...Whatever.*

"Construction work ain't for sissies," Michael
said.

Leroy nodded, though he hated the word "sissy."
He couldn't help but associate it with the surgery he
had suffered as a teenager.

"I'm tired, man," Michael rested his head on the
table spotted with specks of coffee, guacamole salsa
and grease. They were having lunch at The Taos Diner
and the air was thick with the smells of refried beans,
enchiladas and flour tortillas.

Damian nodded. "Me too. There is no future in
this *pinche* town."

"I thought that when I finished high school things
were going to change," Leroy said. He was the only
one who hadn't dropped out. "But they are worse now,
ese."

"No fun," Michael spoke without looking up. "No excitement, no money, no nada."

They stayed silent while the enchilada sauce solidified on their plates.

"I'm joining the Army," Michael said.

The others didn't answer; not immediately at least, but they all felt as if the dim Taos Diner room had been engulfed by a burst of light. The following week Damian, Michael and Leroy went to see a recruiter in Albuquerque and the enlistment process began.

"Army, *carajo*!" Paula Paraíso barked upon hearing the news. "You kids are crazy! Don't do anything without talking to Uncle Chuy first."

Michael and Leroy had lost their father when they were in grade school. ("Lost" was the word that Paula Paraíso used when she mentioned her husband's desertion.) José Paraíso had vanished without a trace, never sent them one penny and lived *la vida loca* somewhere in California. He was a big *cabrón*, Paula said, a bastard in all the sense of the word. She had burned all of José's pictures and his sons didn't even remember what he looked like. The few times they asked about his whereabouts, their mother had snapped, "You guys miss him or what? Go and find the damned old pig and live with him... if he wants you, which I personally doubt."

Uncle Chuy, Paula's brother, had taken up the

paternal role. He had a knack for telling stories, a small moustache and a long, grayish ponytail. He had lived in Mazatlán, Machu Picchu, Sedona and Ojai and became a disciple of Ram Dass after coming back to New Mexico. He claimed that he could hear the Taos hum. Some considered him an *iluminado*; his sister said that he was nuts.

Only Leroy was curious enough to ask about his trips, both physical and psychedelic, and his beliefs, which Paula Paraíso referred to as spiritual mumbo jumbo. Uncle Chuy loaned his nephew *The Autobiography of a Yogi, Baghavad Gita* and a variety of books that expanded his mind (his consciousness, the old man said) beyond the narrow, dusty borders of Taos. He owned a store where he sold turquoise jewelry, Concho belts, sage smudge sticks, incense, New Age books, Tarot cards, and the inevitable retablos and bultos that he made in his shop. An artist with a twist, he liked to give the faces of his saints a distinctive countenance—they were either smiling or grimacing or smirking, but never serious or serene. "My *santos* are alive," he boasted. "They have moods, just like us."

The store's name was The Astral Post but people knew it as Santero's, the name they used for Uncle Chuy though he did not like it.

"Santero, *ese*," his buddies called him.

That puzzled Damian, whose grandfather was Cuban. "The only Cuban living in this crazy, dry and

141

God-forgotten town," he would say with a mix of pride
and gloom. He longed to see Cuba, but wouldn't go
back because of Castro. And he missed Miami, but
his wife, a Taoseña with an attitude, wouldn't live in
that humid, crowded city where people confused chiles
with green peppers, *los estúpidos*.

A santero, for Cubans, was a practitioner of
Santeria, a believer on the African gods known as
orishas. But Michael and Leroy explained to Damian
that a santero in New Mexico was a maker of santos.
"Simple, *ese*. We don't have no *orishas* here," Michael
laughed. "Only Uncle Chuy's bultos."

*Now, not all saints are created equal,
comprendes? There are the bultos, which are
the santos as such. They are wood carved, three
dimensional esculturas. I've made hundreds of them
and I make them by hand, everything. I use piñón
sap to get the varnish and prepare my own gesso from
scratch, too. I am not buying any made-in-China crap
for my bultos. No, señor.*

Michael wouldn't have paid three pennies for
Uncle Chuy's santos, much less his opinions. He
informed his mother that Santero knew as much
about war as he did quilting. But Leroy's resolution
started to melt. Once the initial excitement vanished,
he reconsidered his reasons for joining the Army and
they looked as nebulous as the early morning fog that

veiled the Sangre de Cristo Mountains.

Combat training sounded exciting, yes, but what if he was deployed to Iraq right away? And where was Iraq, after all? He couldn't locate the country on a map if his life depended on it. He didn't know how to shoot. Michael liked to go hunting, but Leroy had always felt an unexplainable aversion to José Paraíso's rusty rifle. The fact that his mother didn't want him to enlist also weighed in heavily. Leroy didn't dare to stand up to her—in truth, few people did. Paula Paraíso had long black hair that she kept in a spinster's bun, imperious eyes and the sweetness of a drill sergeant. When her children were little, she often chased them around with a broom. *"La escoba!"* she would yell when they misbehaved. "Where is the *escoba*? I'm gonna break it on your *pinche* asses!" But hard stares and the curling of her upper lip was generally all she needed to keep her offspring in line.

"Go and talk to Uncle Chuy," she said again. "He may be half crazy, but he still knows stuff. Listen to him."

Uncle Cluy's home was behind The Astral Post. The casita, all eight hundred square feet of it, reeked of sandal incense mixed with piñón coffee and the paints that Santero used. Though he produced the customary images of San Pascual Bailón, San Francisco de Asís and the ever-present Virgin of Guadalupe, Uncle Chuy had a *specialty*; he created tailor-made Jesuscristos, Jesus Christs of all ways of

143

life. He carved firemen, priests, surgeons, mechanics and even baseball players—of the San Diego Padres, no less—hanging from crosses in uniforms, gowns or overalls. Paula Paraíso refused to display them in her house. "Who has ever seen Christ with a baseball cap? That's blasphemy, *hombre*!"

When the young men came in Uncle Chuy was, *milagro* of all miracles, sitting in front of his computer. He sometimes resorted to the Internet for tracking orders, but wasn't fond of it.

"I know," he said, skipping any formal greetings. "I know you want to go and play war. But let me show you something."

He pointed to the screen. Leroy couldn't believe that Santero had been playing a video game. Was it Grand Theft Auto? Gundam Crossfire? He didn't recognize the avatar in red that stood defiantly in a green field, surrounded by defeated enemies. Uncle Chuy grabbed the mouse—he didn't have a joystick, of course—and after some gunfire exchange the guy in red was also nicely killed.

"See? He's dead," Uncle Chuy said. "*Muerto*. That's it, he went with Doña Sebastiana. But there is no real blood, no spilled guts, no bad smells. He'll come back to life in a minute. You can play this game seven times or a hundred times. Some days you get to kill the guy, other days he survives. But when you kill a real man, you get the nasty smells, the blood and the spilled guts. And you know what? Once *you* are killed, *ese*, once Doña Sebastiana gets you, you never come back."

That was all the light he shed on the enlistment issue. Then he offered them a cup of piñón coffee and started bragging. He was working on a new sculpture, a businessman Jesuscristo in a dark suit.

"With the crisis and all, I've already gotten ten orders. If my sister sees it," he winked at Leroy, "she'll have a cow, *que no?*"

"Adiós, Santero," Michael said.

Leroy stayed with Uncle Chuy. The following day he cancelled his second appointment with the recruiter while Michael and Damian soldiered on. They didn't make fun of him, as he had feared, nor try to convince him to enlist, but the last thing his brother said before leaving for the nine-week training course was, "The Army ain't for sissies, man."

Leroy felt like a mama's boy, a failure. In fact, a guy without *cojones*—what he often thought he was.

This is a bulto of Saint Augustine. Some say he is the patron saint of students, not because he was always a good one but, strange as it may sound, because the guy had a wild youth. He understands why a kid skips classes or gets drunk before an important test. I like to portray him with a book in one hand and a bottle of tequila in the other. I'd also like to put a pretty girl next to him but people wouldn't buy it. Taos is still an old-fashioned town, no matter what hippies and newcomers want to think.

By the end of August Leroy also left Taos and became a fulltime student at the University of New Mexico, in Albuquerque. He took literature, Spanish and a comparative religions class. The latter was his favorite. His readings about Hinduism and Yogis, and Uncle Chuy's comments, which he repeated verbatim, made him sound as the most enlightened of his classmates. Spanish came to him easily, too. It was the language that he spoke at home during the first five years of his life. But Leroy didn't see himself as a Mexican and he certainly wouldn't claim to be "a Spaniard," as a good-looking, dark-haired girl said she was.

"Well, of course, because I'm *española*," she said when the instructor praised her good pronunciation.

"Yes, a Spaniard with a *nopal* on her forehead," Leroy snickered. He had encountered the same attitude among some Taos old timers who maintained they were descendants of Cabeza de Vaca in person, though they would write it C. de Baca.

Paula Paraíso was born and raised in Juarez. She was an outspoken, proud Mexicana who called the Spanish *gachupines*—an insulting term, particularly when preceded by the adjective *pinches*. Even Uncle Chuy made fun of the "Spaniards" who identified themselves with their own conquerors. "*Hijos de la chingada*, that's Stockholm syndrome at its best."

Leroy wasn't going to tell Isabella Chavez that she

suffered from Stockholm syndrome. She was rather
pretentious and, as Paula Paraíso would have put it,
she farted higher than her little ass, but he liked her.
He brownosedly agreed that she looked like a Seville
queen, whatever that was. A month after classes
started, the two were dating furiously.

Then you have the retablos, the wood panels.
Too flat, if you ask me, but people like them, or at
least they used to. Once I made a big retablo of San
Pascual Bailón for a woman who had just gotten
married and didn't know how to cook. She hung it
in the kitchen and prayed to him every day, asking
San Pascual to help her prepare yummy green chile
and good posole for her husband. That was in the
fifties, when viejas still cared about cooking well
and pleasing their men. Now the vieja says: Chinga,
cabrón, qué San Pascual ni San Pascual. Cook your
own food or go hungry. And that's the way it is.

Isabella's mother was a classier, taller, Spanish-
style version of Paula Paraíso. Señora Chavez had the
manners of a Grand Inquisitor and the long nails of
a Tang-dynasty princess. She was a court interpreter
who wore tortoiseshell combs and spoke in an affected
manner. She didn't have an accent but *feigned* one.
Leroy suspected she considered him too Mexican
for her Spanish princess, but being used to showing
respect to older women, he was impeccably polite.

"Take care of Isabelita and bring her back before midnight," she would tell Leroy before the couple left Isabella's home, a new three-bedroom condo up in the Sandia Mountains.

"Yes, *señora*."

Floating on the pink mist of their love, Isabella and Leroy told each other everything about their past...or almost everything. Isabella confessed that she wasn't a virgin, though her mother—*ay*, God forbid!—didn't know that. He shared with her his fears of being considered a weakling by Michael and Damian. He admitted that he still felt like a five-year-old kid when he was around Paula Paraíso. Isabella smiled and kissed him.

They also shared their dreams. Isabella was majoring in education and planned to be a bilingual teacher in a middle or high school. Leroy wasn't sure yet. At first he had thought he would take a few courses and then look for a job in Albuquerque, but recently, he had surprised himself toying with the idea of getting a degree, maybe in literature or social sciences.

"That will be a lot of work," Isabella said.

"So what?"

However, Leroy didn't dare to mention that he had suffered from testicular cancer when he was twelve years old. The surgery that saved his life had also rendered him unable to father children, but he couldn't bring himself to mention that in front of his first serious girlfriend. What if she thought of him as a ball-less guy? A man with no *cojones*! The shame! Besides, Isabella might want to have kids, like most women he knew. And even if they weren't planning to start a family any time soon, it was a taboo subject, a topic that was better off postponed or simply left unsaid.

Isabella and Leroy met a few times at a Motel 6 in Central Avenue, but she found it unkempt and ugly; she preferred her own home. They would sneak in while Señora Chavez was working and frolicked on Isabella's queen bed under a stern image of the Virgin of Guadalupe that watched them from the wall. Leroy wasn't fond of that *virgen*—she had the same angry expression that he had seen before in some of Uncle Chuy's bultos.

Yes, hombre, there is a santo for everything. San Pascual Bailón and San Lorenzo are used in the kitchen... I prefer old Lorenzo, you know? The guy had a sense of humor. When he was being grilled by the pinche emperor, he even made a joke about it. He said, "I'm done on this side, turn me over." That's why he's also the patron saint of comedians. And there is el Santo Niño de Atocha, who comforts the prisoners and sometimes sets them free. And Santa Cecilia, patron saint of musicians; once I carved her playing an electric guitar... And Doña Sebastiana... well, she has quite a history, that old broad.

The day of the mid-term literature test Leroy was shaking like a ristra in the wind. Dr. Martin Sanders had a knack for asking about obscure plot details to catch the cheaters who only read book summaries in Wikipedia. Later, as if to make him even more nervous, Leroy's cell phone rang during the test and everybody looked at him.

"Turn it off!" Dr. Sanders ordered, annoyed.

He forgot all about the call. After the test he and Isabella ate at El Patio and went to dance at The Cooperage. It wasn't until the next morning that Leroy heard a message from his mother saying that Michael had been deployed to Iraq. He had nightmares with exploding bombs and turban-clad snipers for the rest of the week.

* * *

By the end of the second semester Leroy was pleasantly comfortable in the academic setting. He had chosen to go to college because he wanted to show his brother and Damian that he could also do something with his life, something that they hadn't dared to try. Michael and Damian had gone through high school wrapped in eternal Cs, and neither their teachers nor their families had expected them to do better. Leroy got a few Bs but nothing to write home about either. And yet, much to his own surprise, he had discovered that he *liked* college. He even befriended Dr. Sanders and read all the novels he assigned, enjoying them in the process. Dr. Sanders encouraged him to take his Caribbean literature class in the fall. "With your knowledge of Spanish and your interest in the subject matter, you will do quite well, *compañero*."

It was the first time Leroy had been told that he could do well in school.

For the comparative religions class he wrote a paper on Uncle Chuy's New Age experiences, peyote and hallucinogenic mushrooms included, and got his first A plus.

Señora Chavez's opinion about Leroy improved after he took a part-time job at the university library and another at the Institute for Southwest Studies where he transcribed moldy documents written by *real* Spaniards, *los conquistadores*.

"The young man has potential," she told her daughter, who passed on the comment to Leroy. He considered it more insulting than complementary, but bit his tongue before stating so.

Then Isabella, who was one year ahead of him, began to talk about commitment. She was going to graduate in the summer and had already secured a job at a middle school in downtown Albuquerque.

"I'll be making thirty thousand dollars a year, Roy! Won't that be neat? We are going to have a lot of money, and mom can help us too."

"You're putting the cart in front of the horse."

When Leroy got letters from Michael or Damian,

who were both in Bagdad having a ball, it seemed
to him, he almost envied them. There was a picture
of his brother with the Tigris River Bridge in the
background. "And I have only seen the Rio Grande!"
The minarets, the Abbasid Palace... How many
palaces had he seen in his life? *Chingao*, the most
distant place he had visited was Los Angeles. Pathetic,
que no? He dreamed of traveling abroad at least once
while still in college, but not with a wife in tow.

"I want to settle down," Isabella insisted. "I don't
really care about signing the papers, but mom would
have a fit if we live together without a wedding, you
know how difficult she is."

"Yes."

"In any case, we've been engaged long enough,
don't you think?"

"Well, we will see..."

His vague answers irritated her. They still sneaked
off to Isabella's house and jumped madly at each other
under *la virgen*'s reproving eyes, but he feared that
something precious, the trust and tenderness of first
love, was slipping away. She would take offense to an
innocent joke he made. She wouldn't call for days.
Once, she mentioned she had gone to The Cooperage
with a former boyfriend. As the semester moved
towards its end so did their relationship, at least in
Leroy's eyes.

"Marriage ain't for sissies, man," he told himself,
bitterly. "One needs *cojones* to get hitched."

He didn't understand her hurry to get married. It wasn't like she needed him; it had become clear from the beginning that she would be making much more than he did, at least for a year or two. He didn't have a profession, or even a fulltime job. He was in no position to take care of a *vieja*, nor wanted to, even if she cooked better than San Pascual Bailón. Besides, where would they live? He shared a filthy three-bedroom house with two other guys and bringing Isabella there was out of the question.

Around that time he learned about the scholarships offered to Latino students and filled out an application for the Thurgood Marshall College at UCSD. Dr. Sanders and the comparative religion professor wrote him recommendation letters. He didn't have much hope, but it wouldn't hurt to try.

Pos Doña Sebastiana...she wasn't always who she is now. She is a newcomer, if you will, in the world of santos. In the old, old days, New Mexicans carried a skull, a calavera, when they buried sus muertos. The calavera was to remind the living that someday they would be dead too, just like the one inside the coffin.

But los padres, the Spanish priests, didn't like that, said it wasn't right to take some poor chap's bones and drag them around. "No, jitos, the calavera belongs in the tombs with the corpse," they told the people. So they came up with Doña Sebastiana. Los imagineros made the skeleton of a woman out of

*wood and put it in an ox cart called La Carreta de
la Muerte. That's how Doña Sebastiana was born
and began to accompany the entierros instead of the
skulls. She is dressed in black and has a bow and
arrows... I've made several Doñas Sebastianas myself.
But she's only an envoy, comprendes? Not the real
thing. The calavera, though, was the real thing. Yes,
times have changed.*

"We have to talk," Isabella opened fire as soon as
they sat at their favorite El Patio table.

Leroy shrugged and pretended he was reading
the menu though he could already recite it by heart.
For the first time in his life he felt a painful, somber
connection with his absentee father.

"I thought you loved me, Roy."

"I do. But we can't afford to get married now, if
that's what you want to talk about. Rents have gone
up."

The waiter came and they both ordered beef
fajitas.

"We can live in my house," she offered after a
while.

"With your mother?"

"Of course!"

"That's crazy, Bella."

"Why?"

Leroy studied his fajitas as if they contained the
solution to all the world's problems in the red, sizzling

sauce.

"Have you talked to her about it?"

"Sure, *mi amor*! You think I would be telling you this if she hadn't agreed? In fact, she is delighted with the idea."

"I don't want to do that. It just doesn't feel right. Let's wait until we can afford our own place."

"When is it going to happen?"

He refused to discuss it further and she stalked off. Her unfinished fajitas twinkled mockingly at Leroy but he stayed and cleaned his plate.

Good and bad news poured over Leroy like May rain on his roof. First, he received a letter from the Thurgood Marshall College: he had gotten the scholarship. He called his mother at once and told her.

"Congratulations, *mijo*!" Paula Paraíso yelled. "You aren't a *pendejo*, you are a smart guy, *que no*?

"*Que* yes."

He also told Isabella, afraid of her reaction. But she lightened up. "Roy! Then everything is solved!"

"How?"

"I'll get a job at the San Diego school district. I've heard they need bilingual teachers over there. Your scholarship and my salary will take care of our expenses. You won't have to worry about anything, just study. I'm so proud of you!"

She hugged him and he didn't have the courage to escape from her arms, her kisses, her joy... He even

went so far as to set a wedding date before the spring semester ended, but he hated himself for that.

"*Chingao. Chin* my fucking *gao.* Why can't I just say no?"

A week later he got news about Michael, but they came filtered through so many sources that when the message reached Leroy it had been reduced to a short, scary expression that his mother mumbled over the phone, "He freaked out."

"What do you mean?"

"*Pos* that he's in a mental hospital or something. They sent him back. We need to go and pick him up."

Leroy told Isabella that they had to postpone the wedding.

"My brother came back sick. I may have to stay in Taos and take care of him. You understand, don't you?"

He knew that with Uncle Chuy around his mother wouldn't need him. He felt gutless than ever for using his brother's illness, that freaking out that had taken place in a foreign land, as an excuse.

"You are backing down."

"I'm just saying we have to wait. I don't know how Michael is doing."

"You are so...so..." She wouldn't pronounce the adjective but made it clear that it wasn't anything good, or honorable.

On their way back from the James A. Haley

Veteran Hospital Leroy kept watching his brother
who was quiet and subdued, eating very little and
talking even less. Paula Paraíso's questions merited no
response.

"How many people did you kill?" she asked once.
"Is that what bothers you? Better them than you,
mijo."

He only gave her a blank stare. Better if they
never found out about *los muertos*, Leroy thought.
What good would it made?

He remembered Uncle Chuy's words which now
carried an ominous resonance: "When you kill a real
man, you get the nasty smells, the blood and the
spilled guts. And you know what? Once *you* are killed,
ese, once Doña Sebastiana gets you, you never come
back." But at least Michael wasn't wounded. There
was no blood around him; his guts were in their place.
Yet what had happened under the intact skull, inside
the brain, in the veins and the tissues that formed the
essence of him?

*Among the things that haven't changed, though,
you have La Muerte. It happens just like this: when
your time comes, los santos take you. It doesn't matter
if you are ready or not. They simply say, "Vamos,
señor," and there you go. They would take you right
off the pot, or wherever you happen to be at that
moment. That's why I try to be on good terms with the
santos. I want them to treat me like family when Doña*

157

Sebastiana, the fake vieja, shows up at my doorstep riding her cart.

"Go to San Diego," Uncle Chuy said. "Michael is young and healthy, he'll make it. And I am here to help."

They were sharing a pot of coffee in the casita. The computer slept its electrical dream of dormant pixels and a smiling Jesuscristo in a business suit hung from his cross. Leroy wanted to tell Uncle Chuy about Isabella and the pressure that he felt about the upcoming wedding, but these seemed like such frivolous things to bring up when his brother was still silent and unresponsive, and hadn't washed his face or left their house for five days. Leroy stood up, hugged the old man and left.

"We have to talk," Isabella said and Leroy thought that his life kept moving in identical circles. Scenes were repeated over and over, persistent and annoying like summer mosquitoes. But once in California everything would be different, he hoped. He had already bought his plane ticket. The wedding had been postponed—indefinitely.

"Tell me."

They had met at the Sub, the university food court. It smelled of fried chicken and teriyaki sauce.

"It's about my mother."

"Your mother?"

"Actually, *she*'s the one who wants to talk to you."

Like in an act of magic, Isabella vanished in the Sub crowd and Señora Chavez took her place. Dr. Sanders' literature class popped in Leroy's mind and he struggled to name a novel. *Pride and prejudice?* Something by Dickens? The professor would have described this scene as Victorian, *que no?*

"You have to marry Isabella," Señora Chavez said. "You promised."

"Señora, my brother is sick."

"I've heard that, and I'm very sorry. But you are still going to San Diego, aren't you?"

"Er...I..."

"Then you can fulfill your duties like a man. What you *can't* do is leave my daughter in the state she is."

"In the state she is."

He repeated the phrase, digging deep for some hidden meaning. Had *she* freaked out too?

"You understand," Señora Chavez said.

"I don't."

"Isabella is pregnant, Leroy," she spoke slowly and enunciated all the words, as if she were addressing a baby, an idiot or a foreigner. "With your child. And if you don't do the right thing, you'll still have to pay child support. Hear?"

"She never told me she was pregnant. And that ain't true. Can't be. Child support, my ass!"

"Watch your mouth, *indecente*!"

He left the Sub without looking back though he heard Isabella's voice calling him. Or was that Señora Chavez's feigned Spanish brogue? *Al carajo* with them! Who had come up with that absurd, outdated trap? Isabella? Her mother? Both? Why? Could she be really pregnant? And if she was, whose child was it? Well, it didn't matter anymore. He walked directly to his car and started off to Taos.

When Leroy came into his house, he found Paula Paraíso in tears. His first thought was that Isabella, or worse, Señora Chavez, had called her.

"I'll see a lawyer," he said, "or call a doctor. Don't worry, mom. It'll be fine. They just don't know… because I never told her… My medical record is all we need to prove I am not—"

"Who is accusing *you* of anything, *pendejo*?"

"Why are you crying, then?"

"Michael! He… he shot Uncle Chuy!"

Leroy's mouth felt as dried as an *acequia* in the winter.

"He shot Uncle Chuy?"

"Yes, he went into the store carrying your father's old rifle and killed him this morning. In cold blood, *Dios mío*, and saying crazy things about computer games and spilled guts and Doña Sebastiana. They've locked him up. What are we going to do now?"

Leroy didn't answer. He closed his eyes and imagined that Paula Paraíso, Isabella, Michael, Uncle

Chuy and even himself had been turned into carved figures. Powerless, frightened bultos trapped inside the wooden prison of their lives, longing to escape.

The Guerilla Girl and The Beatles

There were serious nudity issues in our women-only family. My mother had a nervous illness that Señor Roura, the aging family doctor, diplomatically called neurasthenia. Neurasthenia caused her to shed her clothes as if they were on fire and pace half-naked around the house in her moments of fury, which were numerous and way too frequent. During such episodes, her arms moved like an electric fan's blades and she cursed sailor-style with her breasts bumping against her stomach. Grandma Alicia, on the other hand, refused to wear panties under the pretext that she had only a few left and needed to economize with them. She was a dirty old flasher, said her oldest daughter, Aunt Lily. Dr. Roura, always circumspect, explained that grandma had a mild tendency toward exhibitionism.

A sharp-tongued spinster, Aunt Lily went to the other extreme and wore high-collar, ankle-length dresses that resembled Dominican Sisters' habits. She was a meticulous woman who said "amen" thirty times a day, crossed herself profusely and kept a box of secrets in her closet. The box was full of rosaries, dusty pages with printed prayers and tarnished medals of a variety of saints. Some were counterfeit like a certain San Caralampio that didn't even appear in El Santoral, the official calendar of saints. She refused to be examined by Dr. Roura, so we lacked an appropriate diagnosis for her personal quirkiness.

It was Aunt Lily who burdened me with a horrible Santoral name. I was born on *Santa* Társila's feast day, on December 24th, and Aunt Lily convinced my mother that, if they refused to name me after the Roman saint, she would take revenge. "If you snub *Santa* Társila, this girl will live a sad, lonely and unhappy life," she said. Apparently, the saint never got news that I was her namesake.

Neither my mother nor Aunt Lily worked, much less Grandma Alicia. They were what the revolutionary called "bourgeois." After my grandfather's death, in 1957, they inherited four small houses in a poor suburb called Luyanó and got by with the meager compensation that the Law of Urban Reform had assigned to them instead of the rent money they used to receive every month. As for my father, he had divorced my mother shortly after I was born. I only saw him a couple of times and he didn't offer a reason for his abandonment, though I came to understand that he didn't need one. I would have fled too, given an opportunity.

Following my father's departure, the apartment became an estrogen-filled hole, with three family members in a permanent menopausal state. And yet, hadn't it been for the constant fights and the nudity episodes, our home would have been pleasant enough.

We lived on the seventh floor of an Art Deco building right across the seashore. The open terrace allowed a panoramic view of the ocean and the city lights, and spectacular sunsets filled the living rooms with golden shades. The terrace lacked part of the railing; it had flown away, like a scared seagull, during the hurricane Flora in 1968.

I didn't mind losing the railing. Actually, I liked the unobstructed view we had ended up with. I sat outside and watched Malecón Drive, a busy street that stretched like an asphalt snake toward the west. The constant traffic fascinated me; so did the idea of jumping. A cold hand tapped on my shoulder, encouragingly, when I approached the edge, but I always backed off. The hand went away and the wind growled, disappointed.

My mother didn't take the hurricane's damage so lightly. She tried to have the railing repaired, but materials for the job were not available. Even if she had found them, there was no one to do the work. All the handymen now worked for the state and, as my grandma was fond of reminding her, we didn't have a man at home. But this was a well deserved punishment, Aunt Lily declared. We had sinned against God and decency; as a result, the good Lord had taken bricks, bread, coffee and our panties away. Amen.

The good Lord took elevators, too. There used to be one in the building but it stopped working in

1962 and was never repaired. Che Guevara stated that elevators were useless and morally weakening devices. Since he, who suffered from asthma, had climbed the peak of the Sierra Maestra Mountains, why couldn't healthy, lazy Habaneros go up and down a few flights of stairs? The country needed to save energy and elevators were electricity-guzzling monsters. Out with them!

The framed portrait of the building's owner was removed from the foyer when *El Comandante*, Fidel Castro, announced that tenants didn't need to pay rent anymore thanks to the Law of Urban Reform. The familiar photo of a white-haired man with a gold ring was replaced by a poster of Che Guevara in green fatigues and his customary beret. There had been other, more disconcerting changes. Oralia, a peasant woman who had once been our maid, became the building manager and was given a four bedroom apartment that she used to clean. We didn't have a janitor anymore and the neighbors, under Oralia's supervision, took turns cleaning stairs and halls. But everybody was busy with their regular and volunteer work, plus revolutionary marches to attend so the Floor Sweeping Brigade seldom did its job.

Despite the shortages, the grimy halls and my family's disgust with the government's measures (or maybe because of the latter) I secretly sympathized with Castro and his comrades, who had seized power in January of 1959. I was told at school that a new world had started with the revolution and the younger generation was going to help build it. We wouldn't be like the *gusanos*, the despicable worms who left the country and whose businesses and riches fell to the hands of the proletariat. The old regime was oppressive, crazy and needed to be fixed, they assured us. It was our duty to change it.

If my family was a representation of the old regime, I reasoned, then the teachers were right. I went to revolutionary marches, sang the 26th of July hymn and didn't care if I never got to wear lace panties again.

Many of our neighbors had left the country in the early sixties. They were pretentious bourgeois who couldn't conceive life without elevators, Cadillacs and toilet paper, said Panchito, the president of the local CDR. The Committee for the Defense of the Revolution, known as CDR, was a watchdog organization poetically described by *El Comandante* in one of his long-winded speeches as "the eyes and ears of the people." Panchito wrote detailed reports about every neighbor's behavior and activities, and passed the information on to the political police. His wife, Marcela, was the vice-president of a local chapter of the Federation of Cuban Women. Like Oralia, they were proud and loud communists, Revolution-or-Death types, and had been nicknamed *comecandelas*— fire eaters. *Comecandelas* were more Fidelist than

Fidel and more Marxist than Marx. In fact, their
enemies said, they were redder than *El Comandante*'s
underwear.

"Be careful you don't end up as a *comecandela*,
Társila, with all the crap they teach at schools now,"
my grandma would tell me.

The vacant apartments were assigned to
government supporters: a lieutenant who had fought
with Castro in the mountains, a union leader, a
family from Bayamo that had once given shelter to
revolutionary soldiers...And Josefina, who became our
next-door neighbor after Señor and Señora Morales
del Prado fled to Florida. Josefina was tall and dark
and walked with long strides. She wore denim pants,
guerilla boots and granny eyeglasses. Aunt Lily said
she looked like a *marimacho*, a tomboy. I thought that
she was gorgeous, the most beautiful woman in the
entire neighborhood.

"She *could* be beautiful," Aunt Lily admitted,
"if she let her hair grow and put on a dress once in a
while."

Josefina was a journalist. She wrote for *El Caimán
Barbudo*, a popular literary Sunday supplement, and
had finished a novel about her guerrilla days that
would be published by *Ediciones Revolucionarias*
the following year. She liked to be called Jose, like
a guy. Marcela said that Jose had joined the Rebel
Army when she was a teenager and later entered
Havana riding on top of a tank. Panchito had seen a

.45 gun in her apartment, a keepsake of her times in the Sierra Maestra Mountains. Strangers in military uniforms, Bolivian ponchos and Russian boots visited Jose often. I could hear them talking politics, singing revolutionary ballads and laughing hard after midnight. Other than that, Jose didn't spend much time at home. She was a *callejera*, Aunt Lily whispered, a wild, street-loving girl.

She didn't like to cook either, Panchito had found out. (He sniffed around doors at lunch and dinnertime to make sure that no one was frying steaks when only chicken or tilapia had been distributed through the ration card.) Jose lived off *napolitanas*, the cheese pizzas sold in *La Mosca Alegre*. The cafeteria's original name was *La Moza Alegre* (The Happy Lass) but people changed it to *La Mosca Alegre* (The Happy Fly) after a buzzing, winged army took over the place as the guerrillas did Havana. The Floor Sweeping Brigade didn't work hard there either.

Jose's columns appeared in *El Caimán Barbudo* once a week. I read all her articles, assimilating concepts like "the mission of the comrade-artist," "the tenets of socialist realism" and "Bertolt Brecht's aesthetic," which I later repeated in the Marxism classes that had just been incorporated to the high school courses. (I quoted *El Caimán Barbudo* so much that the Marxism teacher once asked me if I came from a revolutionary family. If she had only known!) My mother shot me reproachful glances when she saw absorbed in the paper while Grandma Alicia wondered if I was being brainwashed at school...

The fact that Jose was a *woman* journalist enthralled me as much as her shiny short hair and powerful long legs. All the other journalists I had heard of were men. There was Cabrera Infante, who signed his chronicles as Cain. And Rivero, the former editor-in-chief of the newspaper *La Marina*, recently closed down by the government. And that American, Herbert Matthews, who had written about *El Comandante* and interviewed him in the mountains. But women journalists? No, *señor*.

Well, there were the columnists with frosted hair, tight smiles and loads of make-up who delivered the prudish "Advice to a new bride" and the insipid "Tasty family meals" in *Vanidades*, my mother's favorite magazine. And there was Jose, an androgynous being with a pen in one hand and a .45 gun in the other. She was as far from *Vanidades'* topics as Aunt Lily from the nightclub scene. Because of all that, I was in love with her. But I didn't have a name for the weird feeling that made my hands sweat and my ears buzz when she walked by me with her commanding, graceful gait.

My buddy Alberto was the only one who knew I had a crush on Jose. We attended the same high school and hung out so often that our classmates thought we were boyfriend and girlfriend. But Alberto wasn't interested in girls—*yet*, he maintained—and I didn't like boys. I liked Jose.

169

Through the sixties and seventies the cultural commissaries regarded The Beatles as the embodiment of a consumerist society that wasted time with rock-and-roll and pot while the *true* revolutionary cut cane in the Cuban fields or fought in the Andean guerrillas. The Beatles were banned and ubiquitous, outwardly despised and secretly adored. Even Young Communists like Jose listened to them. From our terrace I heard her sing *Don't let me down* and *Rain*. But Panchito and other *comecandelas* believed that The Beatles music was a time bomb the imperialists were planting in the Cuban youth's brains.

The bomb exploded when Jose devoted three paragraphs to the band in *El Caimán Barbudo*. A brief piece about their songs and the impact they had had internationally, it was objective and devoid of praise, but also lacked criticism. The article created a tsunami of political wrath that killed her career and made even high-raking heads roll. The editor-in-chief of *El Caimán Barbudo* was fired because he had approved the column's publication. Jose was expelled from the Young Communist League because she had betrayed the revolution in the ideological battle that was fought all over the world. *Ediciones Revolucionarias* announced that they would not print her novel. News of the scandal even reached our building, where no one except Jose belonged to literary circles. Marcela, leading a bunch of stirred *comecandelas*, knocked on the disgraced journalist's door. When Jose came out, Oralia slapped her.

"Now go and write more pro-Yankee crap, traitor!"

The granny eyeglasses fell off Jose's pale face and she hurried to close the door. She didn't even try to defend herself.

Marcela, Oralia and the rest of the gang left singing revolutionary slogans. A copy of Jose's article, torn and covered in excrement, lay on the floor. Alberto and I had watched the scene from a corner, hiding behind a 26th of July flag.

"Jose should have shot the damned *viejas*," Alberto whispered.

I agreed.

The next Marxism class, I stayed mute. I still believed in the revolution but was trying hard to understand how it worked.

Alberto and I borrowed The Beatles LPs from other clandestine admirers. My favorite was *Paperback Writer*. Alberto's was *Let It Be*. We learned to tune in stations on my mother's Motorola radio. Living so close to the ocean helped; Miami's programs could be heard as clearly as if they were broadcasted from the Havana Libre Hotel, formerly a Hilton, which was three miles away.

I didn't find Jose's columns in *El Caimán Barbudo* anymore and stopped buying it. It was so unfair, I thought. She hadn't done anything wrong. She was not a *gusana*, like Señor and Señora Morales del Prado, or a closed-minded bourgeois like my own relatives. She was a former rebel, a comrade. Why was she punished for writing about songs that everybody listened to?

"She should be allowed to continue writing, even if only about old Bertolt Brecht," I said to Alberto.

"But how can she write, silly, when her glasses were busted?"

He wasn't trying to be funny. Getting a new pair of eyeglasses could take up to nine months. There was only one eyeglass factory left in Havana and most of its employees were working in the fields. All over the country, industrial production had been virtually paralyzed. It was 1970, the year of the Ten Million Ton Sugar Harvest. Secretaries, engineers, mechanics, nurses, doctors, bus drivers, soldiers, teachers, and high school students had been sent to the sugarcane fields to achieve *El Comandante*'s goal—ten million tons of sugar, two million more than in the last "capitalist" harvest. The ideological battle was now fought in the Cuban fields.

"If Josefina had volunteered to cut cane, there would be hope for her," Marcela told my grandma. "But she refused to go and hasn't yet apologized for her stupid piece. That girl is crazy!"

"That's what happens when women learn to write and forget how to cook," Grandma Alicia replied, winking and spreading her legs. "They lose their little minds, *verdad?*"

I lowered my eyes to avoid the sight of her gray-haired, exposed vulva. The old and the new regime didn't look, sound or smell too differently anymore. I felt like spitting on both.

By then few people visited Jose's apartment, as if she had suddenly developed a contagious disease. Panchito said that she still didn't cook though The Happy Fly had been closed (the waiters and the cooks were cutting cane) and there was no other place to buy pizzas, or anything else, in the vicinity. But she continued listening to The Beatles and kept the volume loud enough for me to hear them too. It was an old cassette that made a screeching sound in the middle of *And I love her*.

One day I prepared a cheese sandwich and stopped in front of her apartment. "Hi, Jose, I brought you this," I planned to say with my best smile. "Sorry it isn't a *napolitana*. By the way, I really like The Beatles. Would you mind—?"

But Jose had become a hermit. "Get lost, *carajo*!" she would say in a raspy voice, behind the closed door, when someone knocked on it. I couldn't muster enough courage to reach to her. The fear of being rejected was stronger than my interest in The Beatles and my shy crush.

Jose died the same week Fidel Castro admitted in a public speech that, despite the people's efforts and sacrifices, the harvest hadn't reached the expected ten million sugarcane tons. But that didn't matter, *El Comandante* explained, because the revolution would turn the failure into a victory. His phrase became a slogan written with flashy red letters on billboards, walls, textbooks and murals. The cane-cutters had lost their battle but Castro had won his.

We were watching the speech on TV when the stench hit us. At first I thought it came from the kitchen, but the trashcan wasn't full and it didn't contain any offensive leftovers. When I complained, my mother, who upon hearing that our monthly rations of sugar and rice were going to be reduced even more had shed her blouse in a rage, ordered me to shut up.

"Close your mouth and the odor will go away!" she screamed.

An hour later, with the speech still in full swing, Grandma Alicia sniffed the air and said, "Something does smell bad here, you know."

Aunt Lily nodded, "Yes, like rotten flowers."

Then followed a demented chorus because we are ready to face the imperialism it stinks in order to keep our sovereignty but it isn't the garbage socialist can does the damned Cuban people want me pigs are to resign insufferable shut up no Fidel stay forever Fidel shit.

The stench didn't wear off. It got worse with every day that passed and took over the building like a pestilent army. Realizing that it came from Jose's apartment, Panchito called the police. He claimed that she had fled the country after planting a toxic bomb in her living room.

"Sabotage, sabotage!" he repeated, nervously pacing up and down the halls.

"I have seen many worms become beautiful butterflies," Marcela said, "but this is the first time I see a young revolutionary turned into a filthy little worm."

The cops didn't appreciate her figure of speech. After kicking down Jose's door they found her decomposed body lying right there, in a pool of dried blood. She had shot herself in the head with her .45 gun.

"She looked like Jell-O," Alberto told me later. "More liquid than solid and stank to high heavens."

That summer of the failed sugarcane harvest, temperatures in Havana reached 95 degrees Fahrenheit.

I entered Jose's apartment after the corpse was retrieved. Several neighbors were hanging around, gossiping and probably looking for something to steal. The Beatles cassette lay on a chipped dining room table. I could have taken it, but I did not. I took only Jose's eyeglasses, held together by scotch tape and abandoned on the counter.

Later in the evening I offered the eyeglasses to the asphalt snake that meandered under our terrace. A military truck ran over them. I stood by the edge until I felt the familiar tap on my shoulder. "Jump, Társila!" a familiar voice said. "*Salta*, girl!"

But Aunt Lily happened to be around and her frantic cries *Társila is going to fall help me Mother of God and sweet Lord Jesus* came from a faraway place while she struggled against the cold fingers that pushed me towards the street.

Dr. Roura, urgently called by my mother, came to see me that night but, just like Aunt Lily, I refused to talk to him. In fact, I didn't talk to anybody for a couple of months, not even to Alberto.

I dropped out of high school. Years later, when it became clear that we needed more money, I began working at *La Mosca Alegre* as a waitress. I didn't make a lot, but was able to take home cheese, tomatoes and flour which I sold later in the black market. As shortages increased, so did my clientele. Even Panchito, Marcela and Oralia knocked at our door at night, carrying paper bags.

* * *

The Beatles aren't forbidden in Cuba anymore. *El Comandante* himself unveiled a statue of John Lennon in December 2000. The park where it stands is now

called, appropriately, John Lennon Park. Cuban
kids listen to The Beatles in pirate copies and no one
bothers them. The only problem is that the granny
eyeglasses in Lennon's statue disappear with alarming
frequency. The president of the local Committee for
the Defense of the Revolution has sent vigilantes to
watch over them. Though a few faithful *comecandelas*
keep an eye on the teenagers with punk hairstyles and
foreign clothes that walk around the park at night, the
thief hasn't been caught.

Grandma Alicia and Aunt Lily died in the
nineties, in the heart of the Special Period. Dr. Roura
passed away too. My mother is interned in Mazorra, a
psychiatric hospital where nurses attempt to control
her neurasthenia with electroshocks and cold showers.
I visit her every two weeks, and never fail to take with
me a couple of *napolitanas*.

Alberto found a Spanish boyfriend thirty years his
senior and moved with him to Madrid. Sometimes he
mails me magazines like *People* and *Hola*. Panchito
and Marcela fled to Miami in 1994 in a homemade
raft. In January 2001 they founded an organization
"to bring democracy to Cuba" based in Coral Gables
and now, according to the pictures they have sent to
Oralia, Panchito drives an old red Cadillac.

I still live in the same seventh floor apartment
of an elevator-less building. I like to wear modest
outfits and I am not married, nor want to be. I don't
go to the Catholic Church, but I am part of a New

Age group called the Cosmic Brotherhood. We are in frequent contact with all sorts of spirits and I haven't lost hope of meeting Jose again in the otherworld. I also keep a box of secrets in the closet, but mine isn't full of rosaries and old medals of saints. No, *señor*. It contains only five fake granny eyeglasses, though I plan to increase my collection under the patronage of Saint John Lennon. Amen.

Seven Pennies for Yemayá

Yemayá, the dark Virgin of Regla, the orisha *of the seas, has many devotees in Cuba. She watches over those who put their lives in her shell-covered, pearl-embellished hands when they flee the island in homemade rafts, boats and hijacked government ferries.*

Malecón Drive, El Malecón, the street that runs along the Havana seashore, gives off a sweet and sour smell. When the day dies and dark clouds wrap up the city in an indigo veil, the Morro Castle's lighthouse winks with its only eye and the legs of the night open to life.

Aurora, Berto and I walked along El Malecón. The street boiled with kissing couples, expectant fishermen, happy drunks and *jineteras* in short shorts and high heels. But we ignored them and marched fast because we were—on a mission. When a cop passed nearby I avoided his eyes, though cops didn't seem interested in us. Aurora and I were too plainly dressed to be confused with hookers and Berto could hardly be mistaken for a lobster peddler or an illegal tourist guide. Short, chubby and acne-infested at thirty-one, he looked like an aged teenager. Aurora was still an attractive woman and her protruding behind never failed to attract male glances. However, her

179

face, prematurely wrinkled, made her seem older and embittered.

We left behind *Fiat*, a dollar-only cafeteria that shimmered like an oversized Christmas tree. Loud music came from it, a song about a pretty, unfaithful girl who, in my humble opinion, moved her hips too much.

When I dance they call me Macarena
and the boys, they say that I'm *buena*.
They all want me, they can't have me,
so they all come and dance beside me...

Well-dressed people, both Cubans and foreigners, waited in line outside *Fiat*. Soon they would be eating hamburgers, baptized as McCastros, ham and cheese pizzas and fried chicken. My mouth watered and I looked up, trying not to think of food. The sky was covered in a swarm of fireflies.

"Such a gorgeous evening," I said. "The only thing I'll miss once I'm out of this damned place is the view of its night sky."

"There are stars everywhere, *mija*," Berto replied.

Aurora stopped.

"This is the best spot. Now, be careful when you go down. The rocks are slippery here."

El Malecón descended gently toward the ocean and so did we. Others had used the same route before; it was marked by cardboard boxes and unreadable chalk inscriptions on the cement wall. The stench of spilled oil and rotten fish became more offensive as we got closer to the waters. Every ten seconds the vigilant eye of the Morro blinked and lit up the rubble floating around—plastic dishes, beer bottles, a flat bicycle tire and dark pieces of wood that resembled headless bodies. Ring-shaped stains of oil punctuated the waves.

"Let's start with the eggs, Berto," Aurora said.

"Which eggs?"

"I asked you to bring them! Did you forget?" she looked ready to slap him. "The spell isn't going to work without eggs!"

"You have soft nerves, princess," Berto flashed his toothy, mischievous grin, and produced a plastic box. "Here they are."

"*Comemierda*!"

A *santera* had told Aurora that if she threw an egg into the sea after rubbing it on herself, the yolk's attraction would pull her body and soul to the United States. A few American pennies would guarantee prosperity there while a propitiatory song to Yemayá was supposed to secure the *orisha*'s help. I had stopped believing in Santeria a long time ago, but my friends convinced me to take part in the ceremony. What did I have to lose anyway?

Aurora searched in her handbag and retrieved twenty-one American pennies that she divided among the three of us.

"Who's gonna go first?" I asked.

There was a pause as thick as the oil stains over

the water. Berto broke it, "I will. Please, look out for cops, fags, gossipers and voyeurs."

He took off his shirt and his shabby jeans. Next time the Morro fixed its piercing eye on him, Berto was stroking his pudgy belly with an egg and singing,

"May all the evil spirits
get far away from me.
Yemayá, help me go
to Miami!"

When he was done, Aurora and I crossed ourselves and whispered, "Siacará, Lord Jesus and amen."

Berto got dressed and placed his egg inside a hole on a rock.

"We'll toss the eggs and the pennies at the same time," he said, "and maybe we all will win visa lotteries next year."

It seemed like the only possibility for any of us to travel to the United States, seeing that we had no relatives or close friends there who could sponsor us. The other alternative was to leave clandestinely, on a raft, but that didn't sound very appealing—hundreds of people died every year trying to cross the Florida Strait.

"You're next," Aurora told me.

"No, *chiquita*. *You* go first. It was your idea!"

"Let's do it together, then."

Off came our jeans and T-shirts. My flaccid flesh did not match Aurora's slender, tanned and firm body. Though she had had a child, it didn't show. She was still the prettiest one.

When I dance they call me Macarena

and the boys, they say that I'm *buena*.

I felt the sting of old jealousy mixed with a vague desire of being… a guy. But we didn't have time for what Grandma Gloria, my prudish paternal grandmother, would have called *cochinerías*, dirty deeds. We began to rub earnestly our arms and chests with the eggs while singing,

"May all the evil spirits

get far away from me.

Yemayá, help—"

"*Tortilleras!*" a male voice shouted. "I'm watching you, dykes!"

Aurora dropped her egg. Startled, Berto stumbled over his and smashed it. The two yolks rolled toward the ocean but stopped just before reaching it.

The spell was broken. Even the waves hit the rocks with anger. Yemayá had rejected our offerings.

"Let's get the hell out of here," Aurora urged. "If that guy tells a cop he saw two naked lesbians partying on the rocks, we'll be in trouble." Then she noticed my egg that was still inside the plastic box, "Throw it, Lourdes. You have a chance, don't you?"

My confidence in the *orishas* was gone, broken like my friends' eggs, but I tossed mine and it sank fast into the oily waters of the Havana bay. I hurled the seven pennies after it.

Aurora was going to do the same, but changed her mind.

"I'd better keep them to buy chewing gum for Tanya. She loves it."

"Take mine too," Berto said.

Tanya was my unofficial goddaughter (she hadn't been baptized). Feeling guilty, I thought I should have contributed to the chewing-gum buying effort. A box of twenty four cost one dollar in the black market.

Aurora put her arm around my shoulders. Berto joined us. We huddled together, staring at the waves while the shining knife of El Morro lighthouse scraped our faces.

Yemayá takes good care of the balseros. *She hides them, sheltering their fragile vessels with her miraculous blue cape. She protects them from the Cuban coastguards, the hungry sharks and the Caribbean waves. Those who don't make it to Miami are added to her entourage of aquatic worshippers. They travel back and forth the Florida Strait, covered by salt, pearls and shells.*

Berto and Aurora didn't live far from Malecón Drive and could walk home. I had to cross the bay by ferry to spend the night in the town of Regla with *Mami*. Aurora said I could stay with her, but it was a Wednesday, the day when a spiritual group called the Cosmic Brotherhood met in her house (Tanya had been interested in New Age stuff since she was twelve years old) and I had had enough weird ceremonies for the night.

"*Mami* gets nervous when I don't sleep at home," I lied.

I'd have rather gone to *Papi*'s house, but it was also too far to walk and, according to new schedule established after the economic crisis began in 1990, there would be no more buses until five in the morning.

Though I only lived with my father during the weekends, as I had done since he and my mother divorced, when I was sixteen years old, his big, cool *casona* in Vista Alegre Street still felt like home. And yet, strange things happened there too. Grandma Gloria, his mother, had died six months before, but her stubborn Galician ghost still haunted the place. I often felt her hand's gentle touch on my frizzled hair, massaging it with an invisible drop of cold cream. Smells of rice pudding and chicken soup filled the kitchen in the evenings, when no one was cooking, and the sound of flannel slippers moving through the hall made me jump at night.

Grandma Gloria didn't intend to scare me; she just didn't want to be left out of the loop. Her worse pranks were directed against Yurina, my stepmother, who would wake up to find her drawers turned upside down, her expensive make-up kit smashed and the bottles of French perfume that *Papi* bought for her at the Capri Hotel dollar shop spilled over her dresser.

Yurina had made her way into the family three

years before, to Grandma Gloria's disappointment. She
was not the daughter-in-law grandma had dreamed
of, after *Papi* got rid of *Mami*. Following their divorce,
Papi had a long-term liaison with Marietta, his next-
door neighbor, a tall big-busted blonde that Grandma
Gloria spoiled almost as much as she did me. She
even put up with her wild son, Jorge *el Loco*. But
when Marietta and Jorge left the country in 1994,
Papi remarried. This time he did not choose another
blonde, as Grandma Gloria had hoped, but a young
mulatica who resembled *Mami*... when *Mami* was
eighteen.

    Papi's curly-haired, dark-skinned second wife was
ten years younger than I. Her presence in the house, I
suspected, had contributed to Grandma Gloria's death.
She seldom spoke to her daughter-in-law and treated
her, in Yurina's own words, as if she were an unpaid
maid. At first Yurina had tried to befriend me, but I
copied my grandma's attitude which of course made
my father mad. "What has the *pobrecita* done to all of
you?" he would ask. "Why can't you just accept her?"

    In short, my family life was a constant soap opera
of the worst, lowest class.

    His absurdly young wife had not been the only
significant change in *Papi*'s life. He had ascended like
a sputnik, transforming himself, once in orbit, in a
capitalist meteor that gyrated around the dollar sign.
My mother, on the other hand, had gone down into the
earth and stayed there, buried and forgotten as the

symbols of communism, the sickle and the hammer, were now in the former Soviet Union.

When the first Cuban enterprises financed with foreign capital were created in Havana, *Papi* quit his job at the university. One night he went to bed as the Political Science Dean and the next morning he woke up a hotel manager for the Cuban-Spanish *Corporación* Meliá. His new office was on the second floor of the Habana Libre Hotel, now known as Habana Meliá. *Papi* changed his name as fast and shamelessly as the hotel did. His Spanish partners called him *Señor* Torres. Fatigue-wearing Comrade Torres had vanished, eclipsed by the *Señor*'s crisp business suit.

Papi was given a car; not the unreliable Lada he had once longed for, but a brand new VW. He had the house remodeled. He bought a Japanese freezer, Taiwanese rattan furniture and a Chinese color TV. Like an anti chauvinistic magnet, he attracted made-in-somewhere-else products and repelled national stuff.

Mami wasn't so lucky. After the clothing store where she used to work was closed due to lack of supplies, she began preparing cornmeal fritters at home. With the help of her mother, Grandma Inés, she cooked enormous pots of *frituritas* every day and sold them at parks and bus stops.

"Hey, fritters," *Mami* whispered to prospective customers. "Three for five pesos, still warm."

She made good money (more than I did at the
university, in any case) but hers was a clandestine
business. She could be fined, or even sent to jail, if
caught practicing such "capitalist behavior."

Mami had also remarried. Her new husband lived
in Regla and she moved in with him. My stepfather,
a wiry, soft-spoken mulatto, was working hard to
start his own business. He planned to initiate foreign
tourists in the mysteries of Santeria and hoped to
be paid in dollars for his services. He hadn't built a
clientele yet, but had gathered an impressive stack
of the *orishas* paraphernalia. He collected jet stones,
Virgin Mary statuettes, divination shells, tin crosses
and votive glasses.

False Santeria rituals were a burgeoning business
in the poverty-stricken Regla community, as successful
and profitable as the *corporaciones* in Havana. Self-
appointed *santeros* and *santeras*, who had never
practiced the religion before, were willing to initiate
credulous foreigners—for a fee. Their clients believed
that the ceremonies performed in Cuba were more
powerful and authentic than those held in their own
countries. Many didn't speak Spanish and had no
idea of what a real initiation was supposed to be
like, though most of them assumed, according to
my stepfather, that it involved live chickens. (An
enterprising Regla housewife sold "consecrated" black
hens for sixty dollars, undoubtedly the most expensive
birds in the island.) Grandma Inés, an honest *santera*

herself, scorned the bogus practitioners and predicted terrible punishments for them.

"The *orishas* will understand," my stepfather would say. "These are hard times."

He was right. With every year that passed, money bought less and prices got higher. My monthly salary as a literature professor, that used to cover all my needs, now didn't last more than two weeks. *Papi* had offered to get me a position at the Habana Meliá Tourism Desk, but I couldn't bring myself to take it. What? I had studied all the novels by Clarín and Galdós, plus Latin, Greek and philosophy for five long years... to end up selling weekend trips to Varadero Beach and tickets for a night at Tropicana Nightclub? No way! Without my father's help, the fifty or sixty dollars that he gave me every month, I would have had to swallow my academic pride and get a "real" job—that is, one that paid in hard currency—but, up to then, I had been able to survive.

However, surviving wasn't quite enough. I already knew that it would be impossible for me to get my own place, even a small apartment, or to support myself without *Papi*'s dollars. To buy a Chinese TV set or an electric fan one needed to accumulate hundreds of hours of volunteer work, and fight for them in a people's assembly, where brawls erupted over who had more revolutionary merits. I didn't have any intention of marrying well, or at all. Besides, most guys my own age didn't have a lot to offer either. Were *Papi* to lose his job, or to fall in disgrace (as it had happened with many of his old comrades-turned-managers who had become too "consumerist," according to the Party lines) I would end up selling my mother's corn fritters in the streets of Havana.

If I was "I plus my circumstances" as the Spanish philosopher Ortega y Gasset had written, then I definitely needed to change them. I had to move on, or just to move. But where? My first choice was *La Yuma*. Once a feared, hated country, the United States had become my generation's paradise, a postmodern, made-in-Hollywood heaven whose dwellers played stereos instead of harps, drank Coca Colas and drove cars that resembled spacecrafts.

The last ferry to Regla, a small vessel that people called the Night Owl, was expected to arrive around midnight. It was eleven-fifty. I joined the queue behind a perky brunette with a boy in tow. There were three guys who seemed to be baseball players (one carried a metal bat), a young couple and a skinny old man. Later came two middle-aged women that kept exchanging recipes for a "banana hamburger." This innovative dish was made, they were happy to inform all of us, with sliced banana peels fried in tomato sauce, salt and garlic to make it look, if not taste, like meat.

"A socialist contribution to international cuisine," a baseball player chuckled, but everyone shushed him.

"*Mijo*, watch your mouth!" the woman said. "I want to sleep at home, not at a police station."

Five minutes later, oddly punctual, the ferry docked. The captain jumped out and shook hands with the baseball players. They walked away and talked for a while in low voices. When they came back, the captain addressed us, "Comrades, I don't think I have enough gas to get to Regla. I'm going to try, but I recommend that you guys wait here until tomorrow."

His words were met with enraged comments:

"You're crazy, man! I've already been waiting for an hour!"

"If you are going to 'try,' we'll do the same. *No jodas*!"

Since no one else was ready to give up, I also stayed. The possibility of spending the night aboard, wafted about by the waves, surpassed the prospect of scratching my ass against the hard Malecón wall until dawn. The brunette took the boy by the hand and crossed the dock bridge; the rest of the queue followed suit. A single, moribund light bulb lit up the ferry's deck.

"It's your decision," the captain said. "I don't want any complaints later, *eh*!"

The Havana lights twinkled as if saying good-by. The waves licked the sides of the ferryboat and the trail of bubbles we left behind reminded me of the blue beaded necklaces Grandma Inés wore, as a

Yemayá devotee. An arch of light crossed the sky and sank into the ocean.

"A falling star!" the brunette said, showing it to the boy. "Make a wish, *niño*! Make a wish, quick!"

I silently repeated the prayer that the *santera* had taught Aurora...just in case. A big nocturnal bird flew above my head and I imagined that it would land, after a few hours, at the Florida shores.

"May all the evil spirits
get far away from me.
Yemayá, help me go
to Miami!"

Yemayá is always busy. No wonder, since she receives petitions from aspiring rafters every day. Everyone calls to her: worn out oppositionists and disenchanted members of the Communist Party, serious, established santeros *and wannabes looking for an easy way out...old-time believers and people who would pray to Sai Baba, Yogananda or Zeus if that guaranteed them a fast and safe escape.*

"From here, we go straight to Miami!" the captain said.

"There is no coming back," a baseball player added. "Non stop to *La Yuma*!"

I wondered if that was a joke, like the comment about our "international cuisine," but it soon became clear that they were deadly serious.

"To *La Yuma*!" the brunette repeated. "But… won't the Americans themselves kick us back to Cuba?"

"Not if we touch American soil," the captain replied.

"I don't want to go to Yankeeland," the skinny old man barked. "You can't kidnap me! Go back, you bastards!"

"If you try to stop us, you'll end up in the belly of a shark, *viejo de mierda*!"

The kid began to sob.

"Calm down, *niño*!" said the brunette, caressing his forehead. "When we get to Miami, you can have a big steak, an apple and French fries. And a tall glass of milk for breakfast!"

The child stopped weeping and his eyes brightened, "Condensed milk?"

"Condensed milk, evaporated milk, fresh milk, you name it," she smacked her lips. "Plus ham, cheese, saltine crackers, fried chicken… Haven't you seen the movies? They have everything there! Imagine, *compañeros*," she addressed the other passengers as if she were in a people's assembly, "after he turned eight, his milk ration was taken away. I've tried to buy it at the dollar shop, but it's too damned expensive. Three dollars for a can. Three dollars! One hundred fifty pesos, that's what I make in the whole month!"

"*Mamá*, we don't have a *Yuma* ration card," the kid said. "Will they give us one when we arrive?"

193

I couldn't suppress a nervous giggle. The old man, however, was not amused, "There isn't anything funny about this. Do you realize what you are doing, captain? You are stealing a means of transportation that belongs to the revolution!"

"It doesn't belong to the revolution, but to the people. *We* are the people."

"Thief! I've been with the Communist Party since 1940. I worked for Blas Roca in 1956—"

"And what have you gotten?" the young guy cut him off. "What have you gotten as a reward, besides a kilometer of hunger? You'd better shut up. We all want to go to Miami with these comrades…I mean, with these gentlemen, *verdad?*"

Everyone nodded.

"Then you all are a bunch of traitors! Worms!"

"Your mother is the worm!"

"Hey, stop that!" the captain turned to the old man. "Take it easy, *viejo*. See, when we get to Miami, the Americans will send you back to Cuba with boat and all."

Peace was restored at last. The brunette introduced herself as Julia. A baseball player offered candy to the kid. The young couple held hands and hugged as if they were on their honeymoon. The woman who had been talking about the "banana hamburger" declared that she hoped never to taste or cook such a concoction again. The captain said that his brother lived in Naples. He had left Cuba

during the Mariel boatlift, in 1980. "We'll have
lunch together tomorrow," he said. "After twenty-five
years!"

Optimism, like an electric current, passed from
one passenger to another. Soon we all felt in a state
close to euphoria. Only the old man stayed alone in a
corner, muttering curses.

The glowing silhouette of a bigger, faster boat
split the shadows two hundred feet to our right.

"Turn off all the lights, Pedro!" said the captain.
"Everybody shut up!"

Pedro obeyed. Julia and the other women began
to whisper prayers. I didn't understand at first the
reason for their panic, but when Julia crossed herself
with a shaking hand, I remembered the tugboat *13 de
Marzo*. The ship, loaded with people trying to leave
the country, had been sunk by the State Security
Police in 1994. Even the old man's face betrayed an
animal fear. He knew that in case a government patrol
spotted the ferry they would not waste their time
finding out if all of us were there willingly or not.

"Yemayá," I muttered. "I know I asked you to
take me to Miami, but that didn't mean you had to do
it *tonight*. I am not in such a hurry."

"Hail Mary, full of grace and blue Yemayá, full of
shells," Julia prayed frantically. "The Lord is with you
and Changó is with me and my child."

"Protect us, *Virgencita!*"

195

"Asesú, Yemayá," the old man said. "Asesú, *Virgen santa de Regla*. Please, save us."

"*Ay*, Saint Lázaro," the woman of the banana hamburger said, "I will walk on my knees all the way to your church if nothing bad happens to me!"

"I said shut up, *carajo*!" the captain hissed.

The engine had also been turned off. The other ship shone with an ominous glow. Her tall masts and the garland of lights that covered them accentuated the darkness of the sea. We were so close that I could see her flag, but it didn't look like the red, white and blue Cuban flag. It didn't look like the American flag either. Was that a yellow spot in it? No, it couldn't be.

"*Mira, Mamá!*" the kid yelled, tugging at Julia's dress. "It's a corsair vessel."

"Hush!"

"Look at the skull and bones!"

"Shit, the boy's right!"

An absurd hypothesis occurred to me: we had gone back in time. The Night Owl had slipped into the 18th century! Or was it the 16th? I was already feeling like the Yankee in King Arthur's court when an explosion of music and laughter came from the "corsair vessel."

"It's Le Galleon!" the captain said, with a sigh of relief. "Pedro, turn on the lights again. These guys are so drunk that they probably changed their course without noticing."

"Or they want to go to *La Yuma* too," Julia's son said.

"They are tourists, sweetie. I bet there are a few *Yumas* among them."

"Let's get going," the captain said. "The 'pirates' are too busy with their *mojitos*, lobster cakes and hookers to pay any attention to us."

When I dance they call me Macarena
and the boys, they say that I'm *buena*.
They all want me, they can't have me,
so they all come and dance beside me...

The Virgin of Regla listens to her children when they address her with the proper respect. It doesn't matter that they only remember her in times of tribulation. She is always ready to blind their enemies, pull the teeth out of the sharks' mouths and turn machine-gun boats into harmless, aquatic tourist traps.

The Night Owl traveled for five more hours, coughing and huffing. The waves caressed her keel with encouraging slaps and a cool breeze wiped away my fears. When the rosy fingers of dawn lit up the sky, a miniature Morro Castle appeared in front of us: it was a key's lighthouse.

"We made it, *coño!*" the captain yelled.

A round of applause and a chorus of "*gracias a Dios*" followed.

I conjured visions of Coca Colas, hams, mansions with swimming pools and, vaguely, of the intangible,

enigmatic concept that the books called freedom.
Would they all be over there, waiting for me?

*Yemayá's work doesn't end when her protégées
arrive at the Miami shores. She knows they will invoke
her again after they face the immensity of La Yuma,
the land that wasn't promised to any of them.*

Poe, the Professor and the Papichulo

In the middle of her private turmoil, Ellen couldn't avoid recalling the plot of *The Cask of Amontillado* which was the topic of her next class. Ellen, an English professor at the University of New Mexico, breathed literature and sweated grammar. Her students, and even her colleagues, could always count on her to solve obscure linguistic issues and decode literary references.

They didn't know that she hated her language sensibility. When people around her used double negatives or spat *ain'ts* or referred to the *liberry* she would feel nauseated. "But nausea isn't a problem when you sit on your fat butt all day, eating chips and chocolate candy," her mother pointed out once.

Ellen *had* a fat butt and her not so wise food choices had burdened her with thunder thighs and love handles that Papichulo, her Cuban husband, disrespectfully called *lonjas*—slices of lard. There were few things that she enjoyed more than eating a dozen Godiva truffles or downing a bowl of handmade tortilla chips dipped in guacamole while reading a hair-raising story. Particularly in the winter, when the proverbial wind blew outside and the proverbial cat purred at her feet and handsome Papichulo sat nearby, watching his favorite Univisión shows instead of doing his ESL homework...

But Papichulo (whose Spanish nickname, literally translated, meant daddy-pimp) wouldn't sit by her anymore. Ellen wouldn't have to watch *Sábado Gigante* or cheesy Mexican soap operas anymore. She wouldn't help him polish his Cuban-accented, broken English again. After the discovery she had made the previous night, her life, and his, were bound to change; inevitably for the worse.

I must not only punish, but punish with impunity. A wrong is unredressed when retribution overtakes its redresser, had written Mr. Poe. Ellen agreed. She knew she couldn't run over Papichulo in her dark blue VW beetle, no matter how much she longed to do so. She would be the primary suspect because the Albuquerque Police Department would find out in one day what had taken her two years (and luck, if that should be called luck) to discover.

"What a Cuban pig!" Ellen said aloud. "After all I have done for him!"

Ellen had met Papichulo in Cuba. She had travelled to the island with the only purpose of setting foot on the land where Che Guevara (the Argentinean guerilla she idolized) had been buried for the second time in 1997. Papichulo was strolling around Che's mausoleum in Santa Clara, wearing a sleeveless t-shirt that showed his muscular, tattooed arms, when he spotted the middle-aged American and offered to be her personal tourist guide.

"Gratis for free," he said with a sunny, mango-and-coconut smile. "Just because you are so beautiful, *reinita*."

After a brief hesitation, Ellen took his arm and bathed herself in the warm, masculine current that emanated from Papichulo's body.

They kept in contact by mail and lengthy phone calls until she finally agreed to marry him and bring him to the United States. Her mother said in no uncertain terms that she was making the worst mistake of her life, but Ellen didn't listen to her. She was forty-five, childless and divorced and felt that life had given her a second chance by making her cross paths with Papichulo.

Once he settled in her cozy Albuquerque home, the breadwinner role fell upon Ellen's shoulders. But that was only natural, she told herself. Papichulo didn't speak English and it would be a while before he could validate his degree as a hygiene-and- work-protection technician, whatever that was. Ellen began to send money to his family on a regular basis. She hadn't even asked him to work full-time, only to improve his English so he could get a well-paid job someday.

All that, however, hadn't prevented him from betraying her. Her colleagues, and most likely her own students, knew all about the Papichulo's affair.

Everybody had known and laughed at her while she
had had the pink blindfolds of denial and happiness
fastened tight around her eyes.

*The thousand injuries of Fortunato I had borne
as best I could, but when he ventured upon insult, I
vowed revenge.*

Not only had Papichulo cheated on Ellen,
but he had also said that a forklift—a forklift, for
Apollo's sake—was needed in order to lift her off the
ground. Ellen knew she was roly-poly, but she wasn't
hopelessly overweight, at just two-hundred pounds.
After all, she was five feet eight. And hadn't Papichulo
whispered in her ears, back in the Santa Clara
cobblestoned streets, how much he loved her ample,
fleshy *nalgas*?

She sobbed.

Truth had slapped Ellen in the face when she
least expected it. It had snowed the day before and
few students attended her evening class. She dismissed
them earlier and floated on a cotton candy cloud all
the way to the house. Papichulo would be delighted
to see her. He would pinch her ass and call her *mi
reinita*. She didn't feel like cooking so they would go
out and eat beef fajitas at his favorite place, a cozy
New Mexican restaurant called El Patio.

The garage door was still half opened, as it had
been for the last three days. It had developed an
annoying habit—when they tried to close it, it would

come down at high speed and slam against the floor.
Then it would go up again, in slow motion, and stay
frozen in mid air. There was also something wrong
with the automatic motion sensor. Ellen had asked
Papichulo to fix the door, or at least to give it a try
before calling a mechanic, but *el perezoso* had been
putting it off, forgetting it the same way he always
conveniently forgot to mow the backyard lawn...

"No one would sleep with an open garage door
in Cuba," he said, "but here everything is different.
People are so... so nice."

"There are thieves here too, and we're spending
over two hundred dollars on electricity every month.
Heating is expensive, Papichulo, and an open door
isn't going to help cut expenses!"

She had felt so mean afterwards, like a grudging
old hag. She avoided talking about finances with her
husband because his contribution to the family budget
was practically zero.

That evening, Ellen had come in the dining
room through the open garage. The stereo was at full
blast, as always happened when Papichulo had the
house all for himself. (Later, of course, the neighbors
complained to *her*.) A Cuban salsa song, which turned
out to be prophetic, was playing: *Se acabó el querer.*
Love is gone. Papichulo, sprawled on the sofa, had his
back turned to Ellen.

"No problem, Isabella," she heard him say. "See
you tomorrow in class."

Ellen was going to call her husband but a premonition stopped her, a chill that ran through her spine and made her keep still, as frozen as the garage door. Isabella was a tall, slender twenty-year-old student who had once taken a class with her.

"No, I can't make it before," he went on. "My *vieja* has office hours until four and will be around. We have to be careful. What? Come on, babe, don't be so silly. Are you going to be jealous of *la gorda*? A gal so fat one needs a *montacargas* to lift her off the ground!"

After living with Papichulo for two years and a half, Ellen had learned a few words in Spanish. *Mi amorcito* was my love, my little love. *Vieja*, old woman, was self explanatory. (The injustice, she sniffled. The exaggeration! She was only three years older than he.) *La gorda*, the fat one, didn't leave much to the imagination, either. And a *montacargas*— she had to look that up in a dictionary—was a forklift.

Ellen tiptoed out of the house while Papichulo continued the conversation with his new *amorcito*. She drove to The Flying Star in Central Avenue and went on a desperate, calorie-loaded spree, devouring three cinnamon-sprinkled apple turnovers, a Río Grande mud pie and a strawberry milkshake with whipped cream and a cherry on top. Two hours later she returned home, feigned a headache and got quietly in bed while Papichulo remained in the living room until midnight, watching Univisión.

In the morning Ellen smiled and prepared breakfast as usual, resisting the urge to pepper Papichulo's ham-and-cheese omelet with Ajax. *Neither by word nor deed had I given Fortunato cause to doubt my good will.* She didn't go to work. The headache was still bothering her, she explained.

"I'm so sorry, *pobrecita*," Papichulo kissed her on the forehead.

When her husband left, a number of possible reprisals sprung up in her mind like weeds in their neglected backyard. They ranged from a Shakespearean-style vengeance —burning up the house with Papichulo inside—to ridiculous retaliations like scrubbing the toilet with his toothbrush or pouring urine in his favorite wine. The first one was rejected as too risky and the other two because (a wrong) *is equally unredressed when the avenger fails to make himself felt as such to him who has done the wrong.*

Ellen looked at her watch. Papichulo would be leaving the campus now, unless he and his New Mexican *amorcito* had decided to go out together. That day the fat *vieja* wasn't around, Ellen told herself bitterly. They were free.

What a Caribbean jerk! Wait until he comes back. Just wait.

Papichulo returned at three o'clock. Ellen heard the loud hum of his car. That is, *her* car; she had bought it because he couldn't even afford a bicycle. She ran to the garage and her husband waved at her.

"You feeling better, *amorcito*?" he shouted from the driveway. "You okay now, *eh*?"

"*Are* you feeling better?" Ellen corrected him. "*Are* you okay now? Mind your verbs!"

And she winked and blew him a kiss that faded on the chilly Albuquerque air.

"*Ay, vieja*…You can't wait until I get home to start correcting me!"

He parked the car in the driveway and started to come inside the garage. Ellen pressed the opener as he crossed the threshold. He yelled only once; she started laughing. Her chuckles sounded like the jingling of the bells on Fortunato's cap.

A Virgin for Cachita

"Coffee is a great procurer of witchcraft and one shouldn't drink it in strangers' homes."

Lydia Cabrera, *El Monte.*

Martin poured milk in his cup of coffee and kept adding it until the mix became the color of Cachita's skin, a light brown hue. The Chimayó Café where he and his friend Joe C. de Baca had stopped for tamales vanished and he saw instead Cachita's room in Old Havana and her round, smooth face. Her voice also came back, bringing her last request: "I want a statuette of the Virgin Mary, the prettiest you can find."

Martin had honestly tried to fulfill the girl's wishes. Upon returning from Havana, he had looked over an assortment of Virgin Mary statuettes. He had visited the *tienditas* in Old Town Plaza, the Jackalope store and even San Felipe de Neri church, the oldest parish in Albuquerque. But all the images he had seen seemed to him too tacky, ordinary or simply amateurish. He was determined to get the best, only the best, for Cachita. She deserved it.

"What's going on?" Joe asked when the silence became too dense.

"Nothing. I was just thinking of Cachita."

"Is there a moment when you aren't thinking of Casheeta?"

"Cachita. I thought you spoke Spanish."

"*Bueno*, sort of. I don't speak *muncho*... You know what, man? You should just bring that gal here."

"But I barely know her!"

The smell of the piñón coffee reminded Martin of the first cup of *café Cubano* he had drank at Cachita's home. The memory of the curly hairs floating in the dark surface made a foolish grin spread across his face. Joe shook his head and ordered a couple of beers.

The Chimayó sanctuary was the perfect place to get a decent looking statuette of Virgin Mary, Joe had said. He lived nearby and volunteered to buy one, but Martin didn't trust his buddy's taste in art. Joe was a retired car mechanic and now worked as a part-time baseball coach at the local high school. What would *he* know about virgins? Martin preferred to choose one himself.

The tamales arrived, smothered in red chile and accompanied by a bowl of soup and two Coronas. Joe started flirting with the perky Mexican waitress and Martin sulked. A UNM literature professor, Martin often felt intimidated by his female students, more so when they were young and pretty. He didn't know how to dance. Unlike most of his Spanish-speaking colleagues, he had never visited The Cooperage, the best-known Latino nightclub and restaurant in

Albuquerque. Shrouded in yellowish book pages, hiding behind his computer screen, he lived a quiet, safe and boring life.

And yet he had won the heart of a beautiful *Cubanita*. He wasn't as bashful as other people thought. Dipping a chunk of bread into the soup, Martin evoked again his recent trip to Havana. Like tamales in chile, his memories were covered in a piquant red sauce.

It all started when Martin heard about *The Saints' Book of Advice*, a manuscript about Afro-Cuban deities allegedly written by the deceased scholar Fernando Ortiz and never published. The idea of traveling to Cuba in search of the lost book sounded like a Da Vinci Code plot set in the tropics and he embraced it enthusiastically. There was still another reason for Martin's excitement—he had always admired from afar both the Caribbean island and its bearded leader, though he knew little about any of them. The Cuba he was familiar with lived under the rule of a Spanish Captain General, not Fidel Castro. However, he had adopted a few common contemporary Cuban terms, like *compañero*, which he used to address students and colleagues.

"Be careful with what you do in that God-forgotten place," Ellen Cox, an English Literature professor, warned him when she heard of his plans. "Above all, don't get involved with the natives."

Ellen had been married for over two years to
a Cuban guy who had recently died in a freakish
accident. As a result, she had become depressed and
somewhat eccentric, everybody knew that. Martin
thanked her and paid no attention to her words,
though, at that moment, he had no intentions of
getting involved with anybody, much less a Cuban
native.

He requested a special travel permit from the
Department of Treasury, then called the University
of Havana and got in touch with a Cuban professor,
Compañero Gerardo Juan, who offered his help to
locate the lost manuscript. Gerardo Juan had never
heard of *The Saints' Book of Advice* until Martin
happened to mention it, but he didn't disclose that
fact.

Martin devised a tight schedule for his seven-day
stay. He would visit the rural boroughs portrayed in
the nineteenth-century Cuban novels *Cecilia Valdez*
and *Sab*, the primary texts of a literature class that he
had taught for years. He would tour the old sugarcane
plantations, meet co-op peasants and discuss
revolutionary politics with them and their leaders. He
would stroll around Jesús del Monte Avenue, a Havana
street celebrated in verses by a renowned Cuban poet.
The Colonial Art Museum, the Taíno Town and the
National Library were also necessary spots in his
itinerary, as well as Revolution Square, where, if he
was lucky, he could even see Castro delivering one of

his three-hour speeches. Martin longed to experience life in the island. Cubans were probably less selfish and consumerist than his mall-crowding, crap-buying, popcorn-ingesting fellow citizens.

The trip from Miami to Havana was short and uneventful. An airport cab took Martin to the Meliá-Cohiba Hotel for fifty dollars, which was only ten dollars over the regular rate. The following day, when Martin ventured outside the hotel, the hot and humid air wrapped him up like vaginal secretions. Gerardo Juan was already waiting for him in a nearby park.

"The security guards will ask for my ID card as soon as I set foot in the lobby," he explained. "It would take the whole afternoon to convince them that I am not a *jinetero*."

"A what?"

"*Jineteros* are Cubans who do illegal business with tourists. They sell cigars, rum, Che Guevara posters, CDs... you name it. Not to be confused with *jineteras*, hookers."

Gerardo escorted Martin to Jesús del Monte Avenue, a dilapidated and smoke-filled street where big buses called "camels" and a few old Mustangs and Fords terrorized the pedestrians by their utter disrespect for traffic lights. Strolling on the cracked, dirty sidewalks was out of the question. All museums were closed because it was a Monday. They would have to wait until the following day to book a tour of the *ingenios*, if there was one available, but Gerardo advised Martin to refrain from discussing "revolutionary politics" with the peasants, their leaders or anybody else.

"You don't want to get people in trouble," he said. "And you don't want to get *yourself* in trouble. Remember that you are an American. Here, you're the enemy."

Martin protested indignantly. He had always had a high regard for Cubans, he told Gerardo. He even belonged to a Santa Fe-based Amistad de Cuba group, an organization that defied the embargo by sending money, medicines and food to the island. How could he be considered an enemy of its people?

"And how would you prove that to the political police?" Gerardo retorted. "For all they know, you may as well be a CIA agent."

A CIA agent! Martin tried to laugh it off, but Gerardo remained deadly serious.

"Well, fine," he said at last. "I'll be careful."

Gerardo also pointed out that Jesús del Monte Avenue was located in a rough neighborhood and that Martin looked just like the befuddled foreigner he was. Kids of all ages and races ran after him repeating "*Oye, Yuma!*" and asking for money, soap and chewing gum. Martin wondered if *Yuma* was a common Cuban greeting or a bizarre allusion to the Arizona desert.

"What about the *Book of Saints*?" he asked

Gerardo. "When do we start looking for it?"

"Tomorrow, *si Dios quiere*."

As it turned out, *Dios* had different plans.

As the day wore on Gerardo suggested they visit
Café Havana. Martin remembered seeing it advertised
because the nightclub was part of the Meliá-Cohiba
complex. The lobby posters showed scantily-clad
dancers, trumpet players in red shirts and sweaty
drummers. Clubs weren't Martin's favorite spots and
these people certainly didn't look like *compañeros*,
but, wanting to please his new friend, he agreed to
go. Once there, while sipping his *mojito*, he suffered
through Gerardo's litany of complaints, which ranged
from high food prices to the impossibility of obtaining
permission to visit his niece in Miami. Martin couldn't
tell if Gerardo was discreetly asking for a twenty-
dollar bill or help in getting an American visa, but he
didn't offer either one.

"This is the Cuban problem," Gerardo said
from time to time. Martin nodded, though the
conversation was making him uncomfortable. Weren't
people supposed to be selfless and... well... not too
materialistic here?

Café Havana's velveteen chairs and vaulted
ceilings recreated a 50's ambiance. An old *Cubana de
Aviación* airplane was on display surrounded by even
older motorcycles. Benny Moré and Ernest Hemingway
posters covered the walls and the place smelled of

rum, strong colognes and cigar smoke.

A salsa band began to play. The vibration of the steel drums and the shrill voice of the lead singer reverberated inside Martin's head. Intermittently, the drummer let out an ear-splitting whistle and yelled "*A gozar!*" (Let's have fun!) Next to him, a bald mulatto managed to smoke a Cohiba cigar at the same time he shook a pair of maracas and stomped his feet.

Feeling the first symptoms of a headache, Martin turned his attention to the dancers. A white-haired lady's partner was a dark, muscular teenager who could pass for her grandson. A Nordic-looking couple moved every conceivable part of their bodies, except their hips. Three young Cuban girls (a blonde, a mulatta and a brunette) danced by themselves under flashing red and green lights. Despite her well-developed body, the brunette had a round, childish face. She wore a sequined miniskirt and a red top that sparkled like a flying flame.

Gerardo ordered a ham-and-cheese sandwich, an omelet and a daiquiri. Martin was shocked to learn that *he* would take care of the bill—it had to be paid in Euros or dollars and Gerardo had neither one.

"Sorry, but I can't use my pesos here, *compañero*," Gerardo said.

"You mean they won't accept Cuba's official currency?"

"That's right."

"Why not?"

Gerardo mumbled something about "the Cuban problem" again.

Martin tried to cover it up, but felt he had been taken advantage of by his companion. He didn't mind spending the money or paying for Gerardo's food, but the way he had been...set up. He ordered a *mojito* and fell silent. While Gerardo munched he followed, as if hypnotized, the contortions of the brunette's pelvis and the continuous rocking of her hips.

Two Spanish men, over fifty and overfed, joined the girls. Looking at their beer bellies, Martin felt proud of his trimmed figure. Had he been less shy, he'd have joined the hopping crowd. No one cared about dancing skills here; the Spaniards moved like drunken Labradors on an icy pavement.

At eleven o'clock Gerardo wove his way toward the bathroom. Martin sneezed and yawned. He was bored and the headache had turned into a migraine. He couldn't stomach another minute of the salsa, rum and smoke mix. The drummer's invitation to have fun sounded as empty as Gerardo's daiquiri glass.

"Want to dance, *Yuma*?" the shapely brunette, who had materialized at Martin's side, addressed him in English.

"I'm sorry," he answered, "I'm not *Yuma*. My name is Martin."

She laughed. Her caramel eyes glittered like her miniskirt sequins. "You American?"

"Yes."

"Then you are a *Yuma, chico*."

Gerardo came back and shed light on the issue. In Cuban slang, Americans were *Yumas* and the United States was *La Yuma*. It didn't have anything to do with the Arizona desert.

"Maybe it's a mispronunciation of the word 'united,'" Martin said.

"Uh....maybe."

The girl introduced herself as Cachita and told Martin that she was a masseuse. Was he interested in a good, deep rubbing? (She didn't bother to ask Gerardo.) She would do it in his room if he was staying at a hotel, or they could go to a nearby house, where there were rooms for rent.

"Only fifty dollars," she purred, "for two hours. A bargain, uh?"

Martin refused civilly, recalling Ellen Cox's advice. Besides, the mere thought of the girl's manicured hands touching his skin made him tense. As she got ready to leave the table, he noticed two charms that hung from a thin gold chain around her neck.

"I believe this is *Santa* Bárbara, also known as Changó," he said in his best Castilian Spanish. "The other one is Yemayá, the goddess of the sea."

"You know the *santos, Yuma!*" Cachita smiled. "Yes, this is *Santa* Bárbara. The other is not Yemayá, but Oshún. I'm a daughter of Oshún, the *orisha* of love."

Cachita had never read Fernando Ortiz's books

about the *orishas*, but she possessed an empirical knowledge of Santeria. Her mother was a *santera*, she explained, and her grandfather had been a *babalawo*, a high-ranking Santeria priest. Martin invited her to eat something and she accepted. Her order was almost as big as Gerardo's but this time around the American didn't resent it.

When he left Café Havana at two a.m., Martin had spent one hundred and forty dollars and changed most of his plans. He wasn't going to tour the *ingenios*, which would probably be as much of a disappointment as Jesús del Monte Avenue. He wouldn't look for the manuscript either (Gerardo sounded less enthusiastic about it in person than over the phone, anyway.) Instead, he had agreed to meet Cachita at one o'clock the next day, and accompany her to visit her mother.

He said good-by to Gerardo after handing him two ten-dollar bills—all he had left in his billfold— but avoided making another appointment with him. "*Hasta la vista, compañero*," he told the Cuban, and pretended not to notice the mocking grim that cracked Gerardo's face.

Martin returned to his room, collapsed in bed and dreamed of Cachita giving him a foot rub, her Oshún medal dancing wildly against her full breasts.

Oshún is the goddess of flirtation and love.
Honey, amber and cinnamon are consecrated to her. If
you want to win a man's heart, cut off five pubic hairs,

smear them with honey and boil them in the water used for his coffee.

It rained before dawn, a potent shower that unearthed pungent smells and washed the sidewalks. Martin woke up at ten and spent a few minutes trying to understand why he was in that air-conditioned room instead of his Nob Hill condo. He finally remembered and said, "Cachita."

The streets were already dry and clean when he left the hotel, at twelve forty-five. Just as Gerardo had done the day before, Cachita had preferred to wait for him a few blocks away from the Meliá-Cohiba complex. It occurred to Martin that she could very well be a *jinetera* but he rejected the idea at once. She was just a pretty young woman who liked to dance and to have fun. As for her massage services... well, it seemed that everybody needed dollars to solve the "Cuban problem." Being a masseuse was not a dishonorable choice, was it?

This morning she wore a more conservative, almost modest outfit—bluejeans and a brown loose t-shirt—and greeted him with a shy peck on the cheek. They called a turistaxi, a cab that only accepted dollars, and Cachita gave the driver an Old Havana address.

"Petra, my *Mami*, is so thrilled to meet you," she told Martin. "She likes it when foreigners know about our *santos* and show respect for them."

218

Martin did his best to show respect for Cachita, too. He didn't stare at her breasts, at least not as much as he wanted to.

The rundown house that Cachita and her mother shared with six more families reminded Martin of a decrepit New Orleans mansion. Built in the early 1900, it was the ghost of a manor. It had long, tiled corridors and an inner courtyard where someone had managed to park a 1958 Chevrolet that lacked the passenger door.

A strong smell of fried onions and black beans floated in the air. Many doors were ajar and, as they walked by, Martin couldn't help but peep inside the rooms. In a windowless cubicle, a woman ironed school uniforms and a man stared at a black and white TV set. In another room, a young couple exchanged insults while a kid threw a tantrum.

"*Tu madre, cabrón!*" the woman yelled. "I'm going to cut off your balls and boil them!"

"These people are *chusmas*," Cachita said, "really vulgar and crass. Most of our neighbors aren't like them."

A woman who had a towel loosely wrapped around her body (and nothing else on) stopped to address Cachita, "*Mija*, if you want to take a bath, hurry up. No water after four, remember!"

She smiled at Martin and moved on, her wooden sandals clapping on the tile floor and the flesh of her arms quivering like homemade *flan*. A man dashed by carrying a chamber pot that left a stomach-turning odor in his wake.

"Water comes in only for two hours every day," Cachita said. "And we have problems with the bathroom, too. The toilet has been clogged for a month so people throw their *caca* to the streets, wrapped in old pages of *Granma*."

"*Granma*?"

"That's a newspaper, *chico*."

"Oh, yes!"

"But you don't need to worry; there is a urinal in my room if you want to use it."

"Well, I...Thanks."

"Here is my home, and yours. *Mi casa es tu casa*. Come in."

Four life-size statues of *santos* startled Martin as soon as Cachita opened the door. Oshún, the mulatta Aphrodite, presided over an altar covered with a yellow tablecloth. Five sunflowers in a golden vase, five candles and a copper pot were in front of her. Toy ships, blue vases and pink seashells rested near Yemayá, the blue-clad goddess of the sea. Changó, god of thunder and battles, brandished a rusted sword and had a fiery countenance. Babalú-Aye, the orisha of healing, leaned on wooden crutches and had a plaster dog lying at his feet.

"*Mami*! Come and meet my friend."

Petra was a dark, thin woman with tired eyes. Squeezing Martin's hands in hers, she led him to a wicker armchair. It had been built for just one person but Cachita snuggled next to him.

"The *santos* are happy to have you here, *Señor*," Petra said. "You may want to greet them. Cachita will tell you how."

Martin had read dozens of articles about Santeria, but he had never been in personal contact with a practitioner or attended a ceremony. He found the six-foot tall Changó with his long, black hair and that realistic sword particularly threatening. To conceal his uneasiness he began to walk around the room, pretending to examine various knickknacks. A photo of Cachita holding hands with a sixty-something man caught his eye. The picture was next to a discolored Las Ramblas poster.

"Have you been in Barcelona?" he asked.

"I wish," Cachita sighed, "but I haven't traveled abroad...yet. My *Papi* sent me the poster last year."

"Is he your dad?"

Cachita didn't bear the slightest resemblance to the red-faced, chunky guy.

"Yes. He and my mother are divorced and he lives in Spain now," she raised her voice. "*Mami*, why don't you make coffee for Martin?" Petra disappeared behind a faded curtain. "And you, *Yuma*, sit with me."

Martin obeyed. Sensing it was the thing to do, he put an arm around Cachita. She smiled and kissed him on the lips.

Petra came back with three small cups of coffee.

221

So as not to embarrass his hostesses, Martin ignored the short, dark hairs that floated on the surface. Water was indeed a problem in Havana, he reasoned. In any case the Cuban coffee, sweetened with honey, was savory and strong.

He discussed the *santos* and their attributes with Petra, but not for long. She had to go; one of her many goddaughters had requested a spiritual cleansing, a *limpieza*, which needed to be done that very day.

"Don't forget to greet the *santos* before you leave," she reminded Martin. "They have brought you to our humble home."

Once they were alone, Cachita offered Martin another massage, this time for free. His blood pressure rose. Cachita closed the door. Martin remained seated, with the empty coffee cup in his sweaty hand.

"Why don't you take your clothes off, *Yuma*?"

Martin began to undress under the scrutinizing gaze of the four *orishas*. Changó's dark eyes made him so nervous that he avoided looking at them.

Cachita glued herself to Martin for the rest of his stay. *Ingenios* and museums were forgotten and so was Fernando Ortiz's lost manuscript. Martin didn't get to see much of Havana, not even Revolution Square, because Cachita preferred to spend the evenings at the Meliá-Cohiba swimming pool or eating in the dollar-only restaurants, and he only wanted to please her.

She was also fond of hotel shops and had a

weakness for La Maison, a pretentious boutique where Martin bought her a two-hundred dollar dress, a bottle of Carolina Herrera perfume and an exorbitant amount of sexy lingerie. His money evaporated like rain in the Havana streets. But what could he do when she murmured, "Only for you to see, my *cielo*," and tongue kissed him?

The affair moved at a dangerous speed. By the following Saturday, Cachita and Martin were engaged, or so she said. Martin didn't agree, but he didn't want to hurt the girl's feelings. It might also be a semantic confusion, he thought. In Castilian Spanish, "comprometidos" meant "engaged" but it could have a different connotation in Cuba. She also said she had fallen in love with him the night they met at Café Havana. But there was more: in a Santeria ceremony, Oshún had confirmed her feelings. Martin was her true, her only *amor*.

Cachita swore she wanted to take care of her beloved *Yuma*, iron his clothes, clean his three-bedroom condo, and cook his favorite meals while he taught at the university. Martin, who had never received so much attention from any woman, hardly knew how to deal with it.

"Do you really want to live with me in New Mexico?"

"What? Mexico? I thought you lived in *La Yuma*!"

"Sweetheart, New Mexico is in the United States."

"Ah. Okay."

Cachita informed him that the only way she could go to *La Yuma* was by marrying him... and why not do it right away? He simply needed to ask someone to send his birth certificate and his single certificate (Martin didn't know what that was) to Havana by DHL. Then they would go to a notary public and become husband and wife, just like that. The next step was to write to the American Interest Section and apply for a family reunification visa, something that Martin could do from his hometown. It would cost around four thousand dollars to complete the process, though the money for her plane ticket might be sent later on.

This was all too fast and confusing and Martin felt that Cachita's demands were out of line. Fortunately, the week had ended and his cash had already melted in boutiques, restaurants and turistaxis. American credit cards, much to Martin's relief, couldn't be used in Cuba. Tears running down her cheeks, Cachita agreed to wait. Before leaving the Havana airport, Martin gave her all he had left—two hundred dollars. In return, she offered him her Virgin of La Caridad charm.

"I don't care about your money," she sobbed. "If I take it, it's only because I need it to buy food for *Mami* and me. But I do want a statuette of the Virgin Mary, the prettiest you can find. Could you send it to me from *La Yuma*, *amor?*"

If you want the Virgin Mary to answer your prayers fast, take her baby Jesus and hide him. Keep him away from her until your wishes are fulfilled.

After lunch Martin and Joe resumed their search, but the works of most local artists made a poor impression on them.

"This one is too discolored," Martin said about a clay statuette. "And that one looks like a fat Barbie doll."

As the last resort they visited a small, unassuming store. Martin stumbled over a three-foot tall bulto of the virgin of Guadalupe surrounded by a floral frame. The colors were bright, but not too flashy and Mary's face had a sly smile that reminded him of Cachita's.

"That's it!"

"Did you look at the price?"

It was four hundred dollars. Martin hesitated, but then the shop owner approached the two men.

"This bulto was made by one of the best-known Taos *santeros*," he said. "Jesús Cortinas, *el* Chuy, who died only two weeks ago. Now his art will be ten times more valuable. You know, it always happens when Doña Sebastiana takes someone with her... Look, look at the virgin's crown! It took him weeks just to complete it. Besides, the Chimayó priest blessed the bulto," he told Martin. "I won't mention that to every customer, but I see by your medal that you are a devotee of *la virgen*."

Martin nodded.

"If I were you," Joe whispered. "I'd send the girl three hundred bucks and a five-dollar plastic virgin."

"But you are not me," Martin replied. He turned to the owner, "Do you take MasterCard?"

They left the store with the bulto protected by bubble wrap.

"Now I have to think of a safe way of sending it to Cuba," Martin said. "This isn't a garden variety virgin."

"You bet it isn't."

"The fall semester just started and I can't go back to Cuba right now. But if I could find someone willing to take the bulto and... well, not spy on Cachita, but let me know how she is *behaving*, I'd be happy to pay for some travel expenses."

"You mean the plane ticket?"

"Yes, and a couple of nights in a hotel."

"How soon do you want her to get that overprized piece of lumber?"

Cachita's home looked exactly as Martin had described it, except for a new Panasonic TV set that had now taken Changó's corner. Joe stood at the threshold knocking on the open door until Petra came out.

"I'm looking for Señorita Caridad Perez," he said. "*Yo soy* Martin's friend."

"Martin who?"

"Welcome!" Cachita came out and kissed Joe on the cheek. "Martin is my *Yuma* boyfriend, *Mami*," she said in Spanish, "the shy one, the professor."

Joe handed her the package, "Your virgin."

"*Gracias. Ay*, it's heavy!" she put it on the floor. "When is Martin coming back?"

"Probably around fall break."

"Fall break?"

"In November."

"What about the single certificate? Did he get it?"

"I don't know."

"Did he send anything else?"

"Only this package."

Petra and her daughter exchanged a rapid glance.

"Excuse me," Petra said. "I have to run some errands. Come in, please. Let me offer you a cup of coffee, *Señor*, and then I'm on my way. You can stay here with the girl."

After drinking a cup of coffee, Joe turned to Cachita and said, "So you're an expert masseuse, I hear."

"I am," she grinned. "Would you like to have a good massage? Only fifty dollars, because you are Martin's friend."

"Well, hell, why not?"

Cachita and Petra had been standing in line for two hours in front of the Maisí dollar shop. The queue moved at the slow pace of a well-fed turtle but finally

227

the women got to the door.

"*Oye, Mami,* these *Yumas* are so tight," Cachita said. "Joe only left me eighty lousy dollars, plus twenty I took from his wallet when he was drunk. He couldn't make it a hundred, *el cochino!* And he managed to stay away from restaurants and cafeterias, wouldn't even buy me a McCastro hamburger!"

"The other *Yuma* was less stingy, wasn't he?"

"But he isn't coming back until November! Does he think I'm going to wait for him eating slices of air?" she shrugged. "Did you see what he sent? *Dios mío,* a piece of painted wood I could have bought here, at Cathedral Square, for ten pesos!"

"Intentions are what counts, *niña.*"

"Intentions, *mierda*! He probably bought the cheapest thing he could find. And he hasn't yet gotten the single certificate...Forget it."

"What about the Swedish guy?"

"Nah... he's too young."

"He's ten years older than you!"

"Too young to marry me, I mean. He can find a wife in his country. The same goes for Manuel, the Mexican."

The security guard waved them in, glancing at Cachita's lycra shorts.

"Isn't he the one who owns a grocery store in Morelia? You could eat anything you wanted and never be concerned about food prices. You could also send me groceries every month."

"Manuel is a flake, *Mami*. He hasn't called me in seven weeks. He's like most foreigners: a lot of *blablablá* when they are here but once they go home, they don't even remember my name. "

"You're right, *mija*. Your best bet is that old Spaniard, *el* Jordi. He has returned three times and bought us a new TV set. You'd better stick with him."

"I will. That's why I wanted a Virgin Mary. I would have hidden her baby until Jordi came back and took me to Barcelona. But what can I do with that big ugly thing? What kind of virgin is it, anyway? She doesn't even have a baby Jesus!"

They stopped in front of the condensed milk shelf.

"Buy ten cans," Cachita told her mother. "Jordi doesn't care if I get fat."

She glided gracefully toward the meat counter and began to check the prices of ground beef. A new, gleaming Virgin de la Caridad charm dangled between her breasts.

At that very moment, Joe C. de Baca was mentally balancing his checkbook to see if he could afford another trip to Havana in the near future. He decided against it.

At that very moment, Dr. Martin Sanders was welcoming his new graduate students and discussing the syllabus.

"During our semester together, we will analyze the

position of women in contemporary Cuban literature,"
he announced. "As a possible research topic, I suggest
that you focus on the improvement of their social role
after four decades of change and revolution."

Also Available from
**PRESS**

General Titles

Sometimes Courage Looks Like Crazy: A Journalist's Story by Kim Bondy, 978-1-60801-058-5 (2011)

Post-Katrina Brazucas: Brazilian Immigrants in New Orleans by Annie Gibson, 978-1-60801-070-7 (2011)

The Saratoga Collection, edited by Terrence Sanders, 978-1-60801-061-5 (2011)

The Garden Path: The Miseducation of a City, by Andre Perry, 978-1-60801-048-6 (2011)

Before (During) After: Louisiana Photographers Visual Reactions to Hurricane Katrina, edited by Elizabeth Kleinveld, 978-1-60801-023-3 (2010)

Beyond the Islands by Alicia Yánez Cossío, translated by Amalia Gladhart, 978-1-60801-043-1 (2010)

Writer in Residence: Memoir of a Literary Translator by Mark Spitzer, 978-1-60801-020-2 (2010)

The Fox's Window by Naoko Awa, translated by Toshiya Kamei, 978-1-60801-006-6 (2010)

Black Santa by Jamie Bernstein, 978-1-60801-022-6 (2010)

Dream-crowned (Traumgekrönt) by Rainer Maria Rilke, translated by Lorne Mook, 978-1-60801-041-7 (2010)

Voices Rising II: More Stories from the Katrina Narrative Project edited by Rebeca Antoine, 978-0-9706190-8-2 (2010)

Rowing to Sweden: Essays on Faith, Love, Politics, and Movies by Fredrick Barton, 978-1-60801-001-1 (2010)

Dogs in My Life: The New Orleans Photographs of John Tibule Mendes, 978-1-60801-005-9 (2010)

New Orleans: The Underground Guide by Michael Patrick Welch & Alison Fensterstock, 978-1-60801-019-6 (2010)

Understanding the Music Business: A Comprehensive View edited by Harmon Greenblatt & Irwin Steinberg, 978-1-60801-004-2 (2010)

The Gravedigger by Rob Magnuson Smith, 978-1-60801-010-3 (2010)

Portraits: Photographs in New Orleans 1998-2009 by Jonathan Traviesa, 978-0-9706190-5-1 (2009)

I hope it's not over, and good-by: Selected Poems of Everette Maddox by Everette Maddox, 978-1-60801-000-4 (2009)

Theoretical Killings: Essays & Accidents by Steven Church, 978-0-9706190-6-8 (2009)

Voices Rising: Stories from the Katrina Narrative Project edited by Rebeca Antoine, 978-0-9728143-6-2 (2008)

On Higher Ground: The University of New Orleans at Fifty by Dr. Robert Dupont, 978-0-9728143-5-5 (2008)

The Change Cycle Handbook by Will Lannes, 978-0-9728143-9-3 (2008)

Us Four Plus Four: Eight Russian Poets Conversing translated by Don Mager, 978-0-9706190-4-4 (2008)

The El Cholo Feeling Passes by Fredrick Barton, 978-0-9728143-2-4 (2003)

A House Divided by Fredrick Barton, 978-0-9728143-1-7 (2003)

William Christenberry: Art & Family by J. Richard Gruber, 978-0-9706190-0-6 (2000)

The Neighborhood Story Project

New Orleans in 19 Movements by Thurgood Marshall Early College High School, 978-1-60801-069-1 (2011)

The Combination by Ashley Nelson, 978-1-60801-055-4 (2010)

The House of Dance and Feathers: A Museum by Ronald W. Lewis by Rachel Breunlin & Ronald W. Lewis, 978-0-9706190-7-5 (2009)

Beyond the Bricks by Daron Crawford & Pernell Russell, 978-1-60801-016-5 (2010)

Aunt Alice Vs. Bob Marley by Kareem Kennedy, 978-1-60801-013-4 (2010)

Signed, The President by Kenneth Phillips, 978-1-60801-015-8 (2010)

Houses of Beauty: From Englishtown to the Seventh Ward by Susan Henry, 978-1-60801-014-1 (2010)

Coming Out the Door for the Ninth Ward edited by Rachel Breunlin, 978-0-9706190-9-9 (2006)

Cornerstones: Celebrating the Everyday Monuments & Gathering Places of New Orleans edited by Rachel Breunlin, 978-0-9706190-3-7 (2008)

The Engaged Writes Series

Medea and Her War Machines by Ioan Flora, translated by Adam J. Sorkin, 978-1-60801-067-7 (2011)

Together by Julius Chingono and John Eppel, 978-1-60801-049-3 (2011)

Vegetal Sex (O Sexo Vegetal) by Sergio Medeiros, translated by Raymond L.Bianchi, 978-1-60801-046-2 (2010)

*Wounded Days (Los Días Heridos) by Leticia Luna, translated by Toshiya Kamei, 978-1-60801-042-4 (2010)

When the Water Came: Evacuees of Hurricane Katrina by Cynthia Hogue & Rebecca Ross, 978-1-60801-012-7 (2010)

*A Passenger from the West by Nabile Farès, translated by Peter Thompson, 978-1-60801-008-0 (2010)

*Everybody Knows What Time It Is by Reginald Martin, 978-1-60801-011-0 (2010)

*Green Fields: Crime, Punishment, & a Boyhood Between by Bob Cowser, Jr., 978-1-60801-018-9 (2010)

*Open Correspondence: An Epistolary Dialogue by Abdelkébir Khatibi and Rita El Khayat, translated by Safoi Babana-Hampton, Valérie K. Orlando, Mary Vogl, 978-1-60801-021-9 (2010)

Gravestones (Lápidas) by Antonio Gamoneda, translated by Donald Wellman, 978-1-60801-002-8 (2009)

Hearing Your Story: Songs of History and Life for Sand Roses by Nabile Farès translated by Peter Thompson, 978-0-9728143-7-9 (2008)

The Katrina Papers: A Journal of Trauma and Recovery by Jerry W. Ward, Jr., 978-0-9728143-3-1 (2008)

Contemporary Poetry

California Redemption Values by Kevin Opstedal, 978-1-60801-066-0 (2011)

Atlanta Poets Group Anthology: The Lattice Inside by Atlanta Poets Group, 978-1-60801-064-6 (2011)

Makebelieve by Caitlin Scholl, 978-1-60801-056-1 (2011)

Dear Oxygen: New and Selected Poems by Lewis MacAdams, edited by Kevin Opstedal, 978-1-60801-059-2 (2011)

Only More So by Tony Lopez, 978-1-60801-057-8 (2011)

Enridged by Brian Richards, 978-1-60801-047-9 (2011)

A Gallery of Ghosts by John Gery, 978-0-9728143-4-8 (2008)

The Ezra Pound Center for Literature

The Poets of the Sala Capizucchi (I Poeti della Sala Capizucchi) edited by Caterina Ricciardi and John Gery, 978-1-60801-068-4 (2011)

Trespassing, by Patrizia de Rachewiltz, 978-1-60801-060-8 (2011)

*The Imagist Poem: Modern Poetry in Miniature edited by William Pratt, 978-0-9728143-8-6 (2008)

Contemporary Austrian Studies

Global Austria: Austria's Place in Europe and the World, Günter Bischof, Fritz Plasser (Eds.), Alexander Smith, Guest Editor, 978-1-60801-062-2 (2011)

From Empire to Republic: Post-World-War-I Austria Volume 19 edited by Günter Bischof, Fritz Plasser and Peter Berger, 978-1-60801-025-7 (2010)

The Schüssel Era in Austria Volume 18 edited by Günter Bischof & Fritz Plasser, 978-1-60801-009-7 (2009)

*Also available as E-book